MW00488119

The Alex Rider books ... nomenon, with rocketing sales in Europe, America and Japan and a feature film on the horizon. When Anthony Horowitz sat down to write *Eagle Strike*, the fourth title in the series, he was faced with a dilemma. "I wanted to write a different book, but one which included all the elements that make the books so popular, which meant gadgets, lots of action and a ticking clock climax." However, this time he has upped the stakes. "Although Alex is still fourteen, he is definitely growing up fast. This book is more personal, with more at stake for Alex. And the last chapters include a revelation that may take many readers by surprise."

Anthony is a popular and prolific children's writer, whose books now sell in more than twenty countries around the world. He has been nominated for numerous prizes for his books, which include *Stormbreaker* (shortlisted for the 2000 Children's Book Award) and its sequels, *Point Blanc* (shortlisted for the 2001 Children's Book Award), *Skeleton Key* (shortlisted for the Blue Peter Book Award as "The Book I Couldn't Put Down") and *Eagle Strike*; *Groosham Grange* and its sequel *Return to Groosham Grange*; *Granny* (shortlisted for the 1994 Children's Book Award); and the Diamond Brothers trilogy – *The Falcon's Malteser* (filmed with the title *Just Ask for Diamond*) and two sequels, *South by South East* (dramatized in six parts on TV) and *Public Enemy Number Two* – to which three short novels have been added: *I Know What You Did Last Wednesday*, *The French Confection* and *The Blurred Man*. Anthony also writes extensively for TV. His hugely popular Sunday night drama series *Foyle's War* is just the latest in a list of credits that includes *Murder in Mind*, *Midsomer Murders* and *Poirot* – it's no wonder that the *Radio Times* dubbed him "a one-man crime-wave". And that's not all – his horror film, *The Gathering*, starring Christina Ricci, is due for release in 2003. Married to the television producer Jill Green, Anthony lives in north London with his two children, Nicholas and Cassian, and their dog, Plucky.

Other Alex Rider books

Stormbreaker
Point Blanc
Skeleton Key

Diamond Brothers books

The Falcon's Malteser
South by South East
Public Enemy Number Two
The Blurred Man
The French Confection
I Know What You Did Last Wednesday

Other books by the same author

The Devil and His Boy
Granny
Groosham Grange
Return to Groosham Grange
The Switch

EAGLE STRIKE

ANTHONY HOROWITZ

WALKER BOOKS
AND SUBSIDIARIES
LONDON • BOSTON • SYDNEY

For M.G.

This is a work of fiction. Names, characters, places
and incidents are either the product of the author's
imagination or, if real, are used fictitiously.

First published 2003 by Walker Books Ltd
87 Vauxhall Walk, London SE11 5HJ

2 4 6 8 10 9 7 5 3 1

Text © 2003 Anthony Horowitz
Cover illustration © 2003 Phil Schramm
Cover silhouette © 2003 Walker Books Ltd

The right of Anthony Horowitz to be identified as author
of this work has been asserted by him in accordance with
the Copyright, Designs and Patents Act 1988

This book has been typeset in Officina Sans

Printed in Great Britain by J.H. Haynes & Co. Ltd

British Library Cataloguing in Publication Data:
a catalogue record for this book is
available from the British Library

ISBN 0-7445-9057-4

www.walkerbooks.co.uk

CONTENTS

PROLOGUE

The Amazon jungle. Fifteen years ago.

It had taken them five days to make the journey, cutting their way through the dense, suffocating undergrowth, fighting through the very air, which hung heavy, moist and still. Trees as tall as cathedrals surrounded them, and a strange, green light – almost holy – shimmered through the vast canopy of leaves. The rainforest seemed to have an intelligence of its own. Its voice was the sudden screech of a parrot, the flicker of a monkey swinging through the branches overhead. It knew they were there.

But so far they had been lucky. They had been attacked, of course, by leeches and mosquitoes and stinging ants. But the snakes and scorpions had left them alone. The rivers they had crossed had been free of piranhas. They had been allowed to go on.

They were travelling light. They carried with them only their basic rations: map, compass, water bottles, iodine tablets, mosquito nets and machetes. Their single heaviest item was the 88 Winchester rifle with Sniperscope that they were going to use to kill the man who lived here in this impenetrable place, one hundred miles south of Iquitos in Peru.

The two men knew each other's names but never used them. It was part of their training. The older of the two called himself Hunter. He was English, although he spoke seven languages so fluently that he could pass himself off as a native of many of the countries he found himself in. He was about thirty, handsome, with the close-cut hair and watchful eyes of a trained soldier. The other man was slim, fair-haired and twitching with nervous energy. He had chosen the name of Cossack. He was just nineteen years old. This was his first kill.

Both men were dressed in khaki – standard jungle camouflage. Their faces were also painted green, with dark brown stripes across their cheeks. They had reached their destination just as the sun had begun to rise, and were standing there now, utterly still, ignoring the insects that buzzed around their faces, tasting their sweat.

In front of them was a clearing, man-made, separated from the jungle by a ten metre high fence. An elegant colonial house with wooden verandas and shutters, white curtains and slowly rotating fans stood at the heart of it, with two more low brick buildings about twenty metres behind. Accommodation for the guards. There must have been about a dozen of them patrolling the perimeter and watching from rusting metal towers. Perhaps there were more inside. But they were lazy. They were shuffling around, not concentrating on what they were supposed to be doing. They were in the middle of the jungle. They thought they were safe.

A four-seater helicopter stood waiting on a square of asphalt. It would take the owner of the house just twenty steps to walk from the front door to the helicopter. That was the only time he would be visible. That was when he would have to die.

The two men knew the name of the man they had come to kill, but they didn't use that either. Cossack had spoken it once but Hunter had corrected him.

"Never call a target by his real name. It personalizes him. It opens a door into his life and, when the time comes, it may remind you what you are doing and make you hesitate."

Just one of the many lessons Cossack had learnt

from Hunter. They referred to the target only as the Commander. He was a military man – or he had been. He still liked to wear military-style clothes. With so many bodyguards he was in command of a small army. The name suited him.

The Commander was not a good man. He was a drug dealer, exporting cocaine on a massive scale. He also controlled one of the most vicious gangs in Peru, torturing and killing anyone who got in his way. But all this meant nothing to Hunter and Cossack. They were here because they had been paid twenty thousand pounds to take him out – and if the Commander had been a doctor or a priest it would have made no difference to them.

Hunter glanced at his watch. It was two minutes to eight in the morning and he had been told the Commander would be leaving for Lima on the hour. He also knew that the Commander was a punctual man. He loaded a single .308 cartridge into the Winchester and adjusted the Sniperscope. One shot was all he would need.

Meanwhile Cossack had taken out his field glasses and was scanning the compound for any sign of movement. The younger man was not afraid, but he was tense and excited. A trickle of perspiration curved behind his ear and ran down his neck. His mouth was dry. Something tapped gently against his back and he wondered if Hunter had touched him, warning him to stay calm. But Hunter was some distance away, concentrating on the gun.

Something moved.

Cossack only knew for certain it was there when it climbed over his shoulder and onto his neck – and by then it was too late. Very slowly, he turned his head. And there it was, at the very edge of his field of vision. A spider, clinging to the side of his neck, just underneath the line of his chin. He swallowed. From the weight of it he had thought it was a tarantula – but this was worse, much worse. It was very black with a small head and an obscene, swollen body, like a fruit about to burst. He knew that if he could have turned it over, he would have found a red hourglass marking on its abdomen.

It was a black widow. Latrodectus curacaviensis. One of the deadliest spiders in the world.

The spider moved, its front legs reaching out so that one was almost touching the corner of Cossack's mouth. The other legs were still attached to his neck, with the main body of the spider now hanging under his jaw. He wanted to swallow again but he didn't dare. Any movement might alarm the creature, which anyway needed no excuse to attack. Cossack guessed that this was the female of the species: a thousand times worse than the

11

male. If it decided to bite him, its hollow fangs would inject him with a neurotoxic venom which would paralyse his entire nervous system. He would feel nothing at first. There would just be two tiny red pricks on his skin. The pain – waves of it – would come in about an hour. His eyelids would swell. He would be unable to breathe. He would go into convulsions. Almost certainly he would die.

Cossack considered raising a hand and trying to flick the hideous thing off. If it had been anywhere else on his body he might have taken the chance. But it had settled on his throat, as if fascinated by the pulse it had found there. He wanted to call to Hunter, but he couldn't risk moving the muscles in his neck. He was barely breathing. Hunter was still making the final adjustments, unaware of what was going on. What could he do?

In the end he whistled. It was the only sound he dared make. He was horribly aware of the creature hanging off him. He felt the prick of another leg, this time touching his lip. Was it about to climb onto his face?

Hunter looked round and saw at once that something was wrong. Cossack was standing unnaturally still, his head contorted, his face, underneath the paint, completely white. Hunter took a step so that Cossack now stood between him and the compound.

He had lowered the rifle, the muzzle pointing towards the ground.

Hunter saw the spider.

At the same moment, the door of the house opened and the Commander came out: a short, plump man dressed in a dark tunic hanging open at the collar. Unshaven, he was carrying a brief-case and smoking a cigarette.

Twenty steps to the helicopter – and he was already moving briskly, talking to the two body-guards who accompanied him. Cossack's eyes flickered over to Hunter. He knew the organization that had employed them would not forgive failure, and this was the only chance they would get. The spider moved again and, looking down, Cossack saw its head: a cluster of tiny, gleaming eyes – half a dozen of them – gazing up at him, uglier than anything in the world. His skin was itching. The whole side of his face wanted to peel itself away. But he knew that there was nothing Hunter could do. He had to fire now. The Commander was only ten steps away from the helicopter. The blades were already turning. Cossack wanted to scream at him. Do it! The sound of the gun-shot would frighten the spider and it would bite. But that wasn't important. The mission had to succeed.

It took Hunter less than two seconds to make a decision. He could use the tip of the gun to brush away the black widow. He might succeed in getting rid of it before it bit Cossack. But by then the Commander would be in his helicopter, behind bullet-proof glass. Or he could shoot the Commander. But once he had fired the gun, he would have to turn and run immediately, disappear into the jungle. There would be no time to help Cossack; there would be nothing he could do.

He made his decision, swept up the gun, aimed and fired.

The bullet, white-hot, flashed past, cutting a line in Cossack's neck. The black widow disintegrated instantly, blown apart by the force of the shot. The bullet continued across the clearing and through the fence and – still carrying tiny fragments of the black widow with it – buried itself in the Commander's chest. The Commander had been about to climb into the helicopter. He stopped as if surprised, put a hand to his heart, and crumpled. The bodyguards twisted round, shouting, staring into the jungle, trying to see the enemy.

But Hunter and Cossack had already gone. The jungle swallowed them in seconds, although it was more than an hour before they stopped to catch their breath.

Cossack was bleeding. There was a red line that could have been drawn with a ruler across the side of his neck, and the blood had seeped down, soaking into his shirt. But the black widow hadn't bitten him. He held out a hand, accepting a water bottle from Hunter, and drank.

"You saved my life," he said.

Hunter considered. "To take a life and save a life with one bullet ... that's not bad going."

Cossack would have the scar for the rest of his life. But that would not be a very long time. The life of the professional assassin is often short. Hunter would die first, in another country, on another mission. Later it would be his turn.

Right now he said nothing. They had done their job. That was all that mattered. He gave back the water bottle, and as the sun beat down and the jungle watched and reflected upon what had happened, the two men set off together, cutting and hacking their way through the mid-morning heat of another day.

NOT MY BUSINESS

Alex Rider lay on his back, drying out in the midday sun.

He could feel the salt water from his last swim trickling through his hair and evaporating off his chest. His shorts, still wet, clung to him. He was, at that moment, as happy as it is possible to be; one week into a holiday that had been perfect from the moment the plane had touched down in Montpellier and he had stepped out into the brilliance of his first Mediterranean day. He loved the South of France – the intense colours, the smells, the pace of life that hung onto every minute and refused to let go. He hadn't any idea what time it was, except that he was getting hungry and guessed it must soon be lunch. There was a brief burst of music as a girl with a radio walked past, and Alex turned his head to follow her. And that was when the sun went in, the sea froze, and the whole world seemed to catch its breath.

He wasn't looking at the girl with the radio. He was looking past her, down to the sea wall that divided the beach from the jetty, where a yacht was just pulling in. The yacht was enormous, almost the size of one of the passenger boats that carried tourists up and down the coast. But no tourists would ever set foot on this craft. It was completely uninviting, cruising silently through the water, with tinted glass in the windows and a massive bow that rose up like a solid white wall. A man stood at the very front, staring straight ahead, his face blank. It was a face that Alex recognized instantly.

Yassen Gregorovich. It had to be.

Alex sat perfectly still, supporting himself on one arm, his hand half buried in the sand. As he watched, a man in his twenties appeared from the cabin and busied himself mooring the boat. He was short and apelike, wearing a string vest that showed off the tattoos which completely covered his arms and shoulders. A deckhand? Yassen made no offer to help him with his work. A third man hurried along the jetty. He was fat and bald, dressed in a cheap white suit. The top of his head had been burnt by the sun and the skin had turned an ugly, cancerous red.

Yassen saw him and climbed down, moving like spilt oil. He was wearing blue jeans and a white shirt open at the neck. Other men might have had to struggle to keep their balance walking down the swaying gangplank, but he didn't even hesitate. There was something inhuman about him. With his close-cropped hair, his hard blue eyes and pale, expressionless face, he was obviously no holidaymaker. But only Alex knew the truth about him. Yassen Gregorovich was a contract killer, the man who had murdered his uncle and changed his own life. He was wanted all over the world.

So what was he doing here in a little seaside town on the edge of the marshes and lagoons that made up the Camargue? There was nothing in Saint-Pierre apart from beaches, campsites, too many restaurants and an oversized church that looked more like a fortress. It had taken Alex a week to get used to the quiet charm of the place. And now this!

"Alex? What are you looking at?" Sabina murmured, and Alex had to force himself to turn round, to remember that she was there.

"I'm..." The words wouldn't come. He didn't know what to say.

"Do you think you could rub a little more suncream into my back? I'm overheating..."

That was Sabina. Slim, dark-haired, and sometimes much older than her fifteen years. But then she was the sort of girl who had probably swapped toys for boys before she hit eleven. Although she was using factor 25, she seemed to need more suncream rubbed in every fifteen minutes, and somehow it was always Alex who had to do it for her. He glanced quickly at her back, which was in fact perfectly bronzed. She was wearing a bikini made out of so little material that it hadn't bothered with a pattern. Her eyes were covered by a pair of fake Dior sunglasses (which she had bought for a tenth of the price of the real thing) and she had her head buried in *The Lord of the Rings*, at the same time waving the suncream.

Alex looked back at the yacht. Yassen was shaking hands with the bald man. The deckhand was standing near by, waiting. Even at this distance Alex could see that Yassen was very much in charge; that when he spoke, the two men listened. Alex had once seen Yassen shoot a man dead just for dropping a package. There was still an extraordinary coldness about him that seemed to neutralize even the Mediterranean sun. The strange thing was that there were very few people in the world who would have been able to recognize the Russian. Alex was one of them. Could Yassen's being here have something to do with him?

"Alex...?" Sabina said.

The three men moved away from the boat, heading into the town. Suddenly Alex was on his feet.

"I'll be right back," he said.

"Where are you going?"

"I need a drink."

"I've got water."

"No, I want a Coke."

Even as he swept up his T-shirt and pulled it over his head, Alex knew that this was not a good idea. Yassen Gregorovich might have come to the Camargue because he wanted a holiday. He might have come to murder the local mayor. Either way, it had nothing to do with Alex and it would be crazy to get involved with Yassen again. Alex remembered the promise he had made the last time they had met, on a rooftop in central London.

You killed Ian Rider. One day I'll kill you.

At the time he had meant it – but that had

been then. Right now he didn't want anything to do with Yassen or the world he represented.

And yet...

Yassen was here. He had to know why.

The three men were walking along the main road, following the line of the sea. Alex doubled back across the sand, passing the white concrete bullring that had struck him as bizarre when he'd first come here – until he had remembered that he was only about a hundred miles from Spain. There was to be a bullfight tonight. People were already queuing at the tiny windows to buy tickets, but he and Sabina had decided they would keep well clear. "I hope the bull wins," had been Sabina's only comment.

Yassen and the two men turned left, disappearing into the town centre. Alex quickened his pace, knowing how easy it would be to lose them in the tangle of lanes and alleyways that surrounded the church. He didn't have to be too careful about being seen. Yassen thought he was safe. It was unlikely that, in a crowded holiday resort, he would notice anyone following him. But with Yassen you never knew. Alex felt his heart thumping with every step he took. His mouth was dry, and for once it wasn't the sun that was to blame.

Yassen had gone. Alex looked left and right. There were people crowding in on him from all sides, pouring out of the shops and into the open-air restaurants that were already serving lunch. The smell of paella filled the air. He cursed himself for hanging back, for not daring to get any closer. The three men could have disappeared inside any of the buildings. Could it be, even, that he had imagined seeing them in the first place? It was a pleasant thought, but it was dashed a moment later when he caught sight of them sitting on a terrace in front of one of the smarter restaurants in the square, the bald man already calling for menus.

Alex walked in front of a shop selling post-cards, using the racks as a screen between himself and the restaurant. Next came a café serving snacks and drinks beneath wide, multicoloured umbrellas. He edged into it. Yassen and the other two men were now less than ten metres away and Alex could make out more details. The deckhand was pushing bread into his mouth as if he hadn't eaten for a week. The bald man was talking quietly, urgently, waving his fist in the air to emphasize a point. Yassen was listening patiently. With the noise of the crowd all around, Alex couldn't make out a word any of them were saying. He peered round one of the umbrellas and a waiter almost collided with him, letting loose a torrent of angry French. Yassen glanced in his direction and Alex ducked away, afraid that he had drawn attention to himself.

A line of plants in wooden tubs divided the café from the restaurant terrace where the men were eating. Alex slipped between two of the tubs and moved quickly into the shadows of the restaurant interior. He felt safer here, less exposed. The kitchens were right behind him. To one side was a bar and in front of it about a dozen tables, all of them empty. Waiters were coming in and out with plates of food, but all the customers had chosen to eat outside.

Alex looked out through the door. And caught his breath. Yassen had got up and was walking purposefully towards him. Had he been spotted? But then he saw that Yassen was holding something: a mobile phone. He must have received a call and was coming into the restaurant to take it privately. Another few steps and he would reach the door. Alex looked around him and saw an alcove screened by a bead curtain. He pushed through it and found himself in a storage area just big enough to conceal him. Mops, buckets, cardboard boxes and empty wine bottles crowded around him. The beads shivered and became still.

Yassen was suddenly there.

"I arrived twenty minutes ago," he was saying. He was speaking English with only a very slight trace of a Russian accent. "Franco was waiting for me. The address is confirmed and everything has been arranged."

There was a pause. Alex tried not to breathe. He was centimetres away from Yassen, separated only by the fragile barrier of brightly coloured beads. But for the fact that it was so dark inside after the glare of the sun, Yassen would surely have seen him.

"We'll do it this afternoon. You have nothing to worry about. It is better for us not to communicate. I will report to you on my return to England."

Yassen Gregorovich clicked off the phone and suddenly became quite still. Alex actually saw the moment, the sudden alertness as some animal instinct told Yassen that he had been overheard. The phone was still cradled inside the man's hand, but it could have been a knife that he was about to throw. His head was still but his eyes glanced from side to side, searching for the enemy. Alex stayed where he was behind the beads, not daring to move. What should he do?

He was tempted to make a break for it, to run out into the open air. No. He would be dead before he had taken two steps. Yassen would kill him before he even knew who he was or why he had been there. Very slowly, Alex looked around for a weapon, for anything to defend himself with.

And then the kitchen door swung open and a waiter came out, swerving round Yassen and calling to someone at the same time. The stillness of the moment was shattered. Yassen slipped the phone into his trouser pocket and went out to rejoin the other men.

Alex let out a huge sigh of relief.

What had he learnt?

Yassen Gregorovich had come here to kill someone. He was sure of that much. *The address is confirmed and everything has been arranged.* But at least Alex hadn't heard his own name mentioned. So he was right. The target was probably some Frenchman, living here in Saint-Pierre. It would happen sometime this afternoon. A gunshot or perhaps a knife flashing in the sun. A fleeting moment of violence and someone somewhere would sit back, knowing they had one enemy less.

What could he do?

Alex pushed through the bead curtain and

made his way out of the back of the restaurant. He was relieved to find himself in the street, away from the square. Only now did he try to collect his thoughts. He could go to the police, of course. He could tell them that he was a spy who had worked, three times now, for MI6 – British military intelligence. He could say that he had recognized Yassen, knew him for what he was, and that a killing would almost certainly take place that afternoon unless he was stopped.

But what good would it do? The French police might understand him, but they would never believe him. He was a fourteen-year-old English schoolboy with sand in his hair and a suntan. They would take one look at him and laugh.

He could go to Sabina and her parents. But Alex didn't want to do that either. He was only here because they had invited him, and why should he bring murder into their holiday? Not that they would believe him any more than the police. Once, when he had been staying with her in Cornwall, Alex had tried to tell Sabina the truth. She had thought he was joking.

Alex looked around at the tourist shops, the ice-cream parlours, the crowds strolling happily along the street. It was a typical picture-postcard view. The real world. So what the hell was he doing getting mixed up again with spies and assassins? He was on holiday. This was none of his business. Let Yassen do whatever he wanted. Alex wouldn't be able to stop him even if he tried. Better to forget that he had ever seen him.

Alex took a deep breath and walked back down the road towards the beach to find Sabina and her parents. As he went he tried to work out what he would tell them: why he had left so suddenly and why he was no longer smiling now that he was back.

That afternoon, Alex and Sabina hitched a lift with a local farmer to Aigues-Mortes, a fortified town on the edge of the salt marshes. Sabina wanted to escape from her parents and hang out in a French café, where they could watch the locals and tourists rub shoulders in the street. She had devised a system for marking French teenagers for good looks – with points lost for weedy legs, crooked teeth or bad dress sense. Nobody had yet scored more than seven out of twenty and Alex would normally have been happy sitting with her, listening to her as she laughed out loud.

But not this afternoon.

Everything was out of focus. The great walls

and towers that surrounded him were miles away, and the sightseers seemed to be moving too slowly, like a film that had run down. Alex wanted to enjoy being here. He wanted to feel part of the holiday again. But seeing Yassen had spoilt it all.

Alex had met Sabina only a month before, when the two of them had been helping at the Wimbledon tennis tournament, but they had struck up an immediate friendship. Sabina was an only child. Her mother, Liz, worked as a fashion designer; her father, Edward, was a journalist. Alex hadn't seen very much of him. He had started the holiday late, coming down on the train from Paris, and had been working on some story ever since.

The family had rented a house just outside Saint-Pierre, right on the edge of a river, the Petit Rhône. It was a simple place, typical of the area: bright white with blue shutters and a roof of sun-baked terracotta tiles. There were three bedrooms and, on the ground floor, an airy, old-fashioned kitchen that opened onto an overgrown garden with a swimming pool and a tennis court with weeds pushing through the asphalt. Alex had loved it from the start. His bedroom overlooked the river, and every evening he and

Sabina had spent hours sprawled over an old wicker sofa, talking quietly and watching the water ripple past.

The first week of the holiday had disappeared in a flash. They had swum in the pool and in the sea, which was less than a mile away. They had gone walking, climbing, canoeing and, once (it wasn't Alex's favourite sport), horse-riding. Alex really liked Sabina's parents. They were the sort of adults who hadn't forgotten that they had once been teenagers themselves, and more or less left him and Sabina to do whatever they wanted on their own. And for the last seven days everything had been fine.

Until Yassen.

The address is confirmed and everything has been arranged. We'll do it this afternoon...

What was the Russian planning to do in Saint-Pierre? What bad luck was it that had brought him here, casting his shadow once again over Alex's life? Despite the heat of the afternoon sun, Alex shivered.

"Alex?"

He realized that Sabina had been talking to him, and looked round. She was gazing across the table with a look of concern. "What are you think-ing about?" she asked. "You were miles away."

"Nothing."

"You haven't been yourself all afternoon. Did something happen this morning? Where did you disappear to on the beach?"

"I told you. I just needed a drink." He hated having to lie to her but he couldn't tell her the truth.

"I was just saying we ought to get going. I promised we'd be home by five. Oh my God! Look at that one!" She pointed at another teenager walking past. "Four out of twenty. Aren't there *any* good-looking boys in France?" She glanced at Alex. "Apart from you, I mean."

"So how many do I get out of twenty?" Alex asked.

Sabina considered. "Twelve and a half," she said at last. "But don't worry, Alex. Another ten years and you'll be perfect."

Sometimes horror announces itself in the smallest of ways.

On this day it was a single police car, racing along the wide, empty road that twisted down to Saint-Pierre. Alex and Sabina were sitting in the back of the same truck that had brought them. They were looking at a herd of cows grazing in one of the fields when the police car – blue and white with a light flashing on the roof – overtook them and tore off into the distance. Alex still had Yassen on his mind and the sight of it tightened the knot in the pit of his stomach. But it was only a police car. It didn't have to mean anything.

But then there was a helicopter, taking off from somewhere not so far away and arcing into the brilliant sky. Sabina saw it and pointed at it.

"Something's happened," she said. "That's just come from the town."

Had the helicopter come from the town? Alex wasn't so sure. He watched it sweep over them and disappear in the direction of Aigues-Mortes, and all the time his breaths were getting shorter and he felt the heavy weight of some nameless dread.

And then they turned a corner and Alex knew that his worst fears had come true – but in a way that he could never have foreseen.

Rubble, jagged brickwork and twisted steel. Thick black smoke curling into the sky. Their house had been blown apart. Just one wall remained intact, giving the cruel illusion that not too much damage had been done. But the rest of it was gone. Alex saw a brass bed hanging at a crazy angle, somehow suspended in mid-air. A pair of blue shutters lay in the grass about fifty metres away. The water in the swimming pool was brown and scummy. The blast must have been immense.

A fleet of cars and vans was parked around the building. They belonged to the police, the hospital, the fire department and the anti-terrorist squad. To Alex they didn't look real: more like brightly coloured toys. In a foreign country, nothing looks more foreign than its emergency services.

"Mum! Dad!"

Alex heard Sabina shout the words and saw her leap out of the truck before they had stopped moving. Then she was running across the gravel drive, forcing her way between the officials in their different uniforms. The truck stopped and Alex climbed down, unsure whether his feet would come into contact with the ground or if he would simply go on, right through it. His head was spinning; he thought he was going to faint.

Nobody spoke to him as he continued forward. It was as if he wasn't there at all. Ahead of him he saw Sabina's mother appear from nowhere, her face streaked with ashes and tears, and he thought to himself that if she was all right, if she had been out of the house when the explosion happened, then maybe Edward Pleasure had escaped too. But then he saw Sabina begin to shake and fall into her mother's arms, and he knew the worst.

He drew nearer, in time to hear Liz's words as she clutched hold of her daughter.

"We still don't know what happened. Dad's been taken by helicopter to Montpellier. He's alive, Sabina, but he's badly injured. We're going to him now. You know your dad's a fighter. But the doctors aren't sure if he's going to make it or not. We just don't know…"

The smell of burning reached out to Alex and engulfed him. The smoke had blotted out the sun. His eyes began to water and he fought for breath.

This was his fault.

He didn't know why it had happened but he was utterly certain who was responsible.

Yassen Gregorovich.

None of my business. That was what Alex had thought. This was the result.

THE FINGER ON THE TRIGGER

The policeman facing Alex was young, inexperienced, and struggling to find the right words. It wasn't just that he was having difficulty with the English language, Alex realized. Down here in this odd, quiet corner of France, the worst he would usually have to deal with would be the occasional drunk driver or maybe a tourist losing his wallet on the beach. This was a new situation and he was completely out of his depth.

"It is the most terrible affair," he was saying. "You have known Monsieur Pleasure very long time?"

"No. Not very long time," Alex said.

"He will receive the best treatment." The policeman smiled encouragingly. "Madame Pleasure and her daughter are going now to hospital but they have requested us to occupy us with you."

Alex was sitting on a folding chair in the shadow of a tree. It was just after five o'clock but the sun was still hot. The river flowed past a few metres away and he would have given anything to dive into the water and swim, and keep swimming, until he had put this whole business behind him.

Sabina and her mother had left about ten minutes ago and now he was on his own with this young policeman. He had been given a chair in the shade and a bottle of water, but it was obvious that nobody knew what to do with him. This wasn't his family. He had no right to be here. More officials had turned up: senior policemen, senior firemen. They were moving slowly through the wreckage, occasionally turning over a plank of wood or moving a piece of broken furniture as if they might uncover the one simple clue that would tell them why this had taken place.

"We have telephoned to your consul," the policeman was saying. "They will come to take you home. But they must send a representative from Lyon. It is a long way. So tonight you must wait here in Saint-Pierre."

"I know who did this," Alex said.

"Comment?"

"I know who was responsible." Alex glanced in the direction of the house. "You have to go into the town. There is a yacht tied to the jetty. I didn't see the name but you can't miss it. It's huge ... white. There's a man on the yacht; his name is Yassen Gregorovich. You have to arrest him before he can get away."

The policeman stared at Alex, astonished. Alex wondered how much he had understood.

"I am sorry? What is it that you say? This man, Yassen..."

"Yassen Gregorovich."

"You know him?"

"Yes."

"Who is he?"

"He's a killer. He is paid to kill people. I saw him this morning."

"Please!" The policeman held up a hand. He didn't want to listen to any more. "Wait here."

Alex watched him walk away towards the parked cars, presumably to find a senior officer. He took a sip of water, then stood up himself. He didn't want to sit here watching the events from a folding chair like a picnicker. He walked towards the house. There was an evening breeze but the smell of burnt wood still hung heavily all around. A scrap of paper, scorched and blackened, blew across the gravel. On an impulse, Alex reached down and picked it up.

He read:

> caviar for breakfast, and the swimming pool at his Wiltshire mansion is rumoured to have been built in the shape of Elvis Presley. But Damian Cray is more than the world's richest and most successful pop star. His business ventures – including hotels, TV stations and computer games – have added millions more to his personal fortune.
>
> The questions remain. Why was Cray in Paris earlier this week and why did he arrange a secret meeting with

That was all there was. The paper turned black and the words disappeared.

Alex realized what he was looking at. It must be a page from the article that Edward Pleasure had been working on ever since he had arrived at the house. Something to do with the mega-celebrity Damian Cray...

"Excusez-moi, jeune homme..."

He looked up and saw that the policeman had returned with a second man, this one a few years older, with a downturned mouth and a small moustache. Alex's heart sank. He recognized the type before the man had even spoken. Oily and self-important, and wearing a uniform that was too neat, there was disbelief etched all over his face.

"You have something to tell us?" he asked. He spoke better English than his colleague.

Alex repeated what he had said.

"How do you know about this man? The man on the boat."

"He killed my uncle."

"Who was your uncle?"

"He was a spy. He worked for MI6." Alex took a deep breath. "I think *I* may have been the target of the bomb. I think he was trying to kill *me*..."

The two policemen spoke briefly together, then turned back to Alex. Alex knew what was coming. The senior policeman had rearranged his features so that he now looked down at Alex with a mixture of kindness and concern. But there was arrogance there too: *I am right. You are wrong. And nothing will persuade me otherwise.* He was like a bad teacher in a bad school, putting a cross beside a right answer.

"You have had a terrible shock," the policeman said. "The explosion ... we already know that it was caused by a leak in the gas pipe."

"No..." Alex shook his head.

The policeman held up a hand. "There is no reason why an assassin would wish to harm a family on holiday. But I understand. You are upset; it is quite possible that you are in shock. You do not know what it is you are saying."

"Please—"

"We have sent for someone from your consulate and he will arrive soon. Until then it would be better if you did not interfere."

Alex hung his head. "Do you mind if I go for a walk?" he said. The words came out low and muffled.

"A walk?"

"Just five minutes. I want to be on my own."

"Of course. Do not go too far. Would you like someone to accompany you?"

"No. I'll be all right."

He turned and walked away. He had avoided meeting the policemen's eyes and they doubtless thought he was ashamed of himself. That was all right. Alex didn't want them to see his fury, the black anger that coursed through him like an arctic river. They hadn't believed him! They had treated him like a stupid child!

With every step he took, images stamped themselves on his mind. Sabina's eyes widening as she took in the wreck of the house. Edward Pleasure being flown to some city hospital. Yassen Gregorovich on the deck of his yacht, gliding off into the sunset, another job done. And it was Alex's fault! That was the worst of it. That was the unforgivable part. Well, he wasn't going to sit there and take it. Alex allowed his rage to carry him forward. It was time to take control.

When he reached the main road, he glanced back. The policemen had forgotten him. He took one last look at the burnt-out shell that had been his holiday home, and the darkness rose up in him again. He turned away and began to run.

Saint-Pierre was just under a mile away. It was early evening by the time he arrived there and the streets were packed with people in a festive mood. In fact, the town seemed busier than ever. Then he remembered. There was a bullfight tonight and people had driven in from all around to watch it.

The sun was already dipping behind the horizon but daylight still lingered in the air as if accidentally left behind. The street lamps were lit, throwing garish pools of orange onto the sandy pavements. An old carousel turned round and round, a spinning blur of electric bulbs and jangling music. Alex made his way through it all without stopping. Suddenly he was on the other side of the town and the streets were quiet again. The night had advanced and everything was a little more grey.

He hadn't expected to see the yacht. At the back of his mind he had thought that Yassen would have left long ago. But there it still was, moored where he had seen it earlier that day, a lifetime ago. There was nobody in sight. It seemed that the whole town had gone to the bullfight. Then a figure stepped out of the darkness and Alex saw the bald man with the sunburn. He was still dressed in the white suit. He was smoking a cigar, the smouldering tip casting a red glow across his face.

There were lights glinting behind the portholes of the boat. Would he find Yassen behind one of them? Alex had no real idea what he was doing. Anger was still driving him blindly on. All he knew was that he had to get onto the yacht and that nothing was going to stop him.

The man's name was Franco. He had stepped down onto the jetty because Yassen hated the smell of cigar smoke. He didn't like Yassen. More than that; he was afraid of him. When the Russian had heard that Edward Pleasure had been injured, not killed, he had said nothing, but there had been something intense and ugly in his eyes. For a moment he had looked at Raoul, the deckhand. It had been Raoul who had actually placed the bomb ... too far from the journalist's room, as it turned out. The mistake was his. And Franco knew that Yassen had very nearly killed him there and then. Perhaps he still would. God – what a mess!

Franco heard a shoe scraping against loose rubble and saw a boy walking towards him. He was slim and suntanned, wearing shorts and a faded Stone Age T-shirt, with a string of wooden beads around his neck. He had fair hair which hung in strands over his forehead. He must be a tourist – he looked English. But what was he doing here?

Alex had wondered how close he could get to the man before his suspicions were aroused. If it had been an adult approaching the boat, it would have been a different matter; the fact that he was only fourteen was the main reason he had been so useful to MI6. People didn't notice him until it was too late.

That was what happened now. As the boy came closer, Franco was struck by the dark brown eyes set in a face that was somehow too serious for a boy of that age. They were eyes that had seen too much.

Alex drew level with Franco. At that moment, he lashed out, spinning round on the ball of his left foot, kicking with the right. Franco was taken completely by surprise. Alex's heel struck him hard in the stomach – but straight away Alex knew that he had underestimated his opponent. He had expected to feel soft fat beneath the flapping suit. But his foot had slammed into a ring of muscle, and although Franco was hurt and winded, he hadn't been brought down.

Franco dropped the cigar and lunged, his hand already scrabbling in his jacket pocket. It came out holding something. There was a soft click and seven inches of glinting silver leapt out of nowhere. He had a flick knife. Moving much faster than Alex would have thought possible, he launched himself across the jetty. His hand swung in an arc. Alex heard the blade slicing the air. He swung again, and the knife flashed past Alex's face, missing him by a centimetre.

Alex was unarmed. Franco had obviously used the knife many times before, and if he hadn't been weakened by the first kick, this fight would already have been over. Alex looked around, searching for anything he could defend himself with. There was almost nothing on the jetty – just a few old boxes, a bucket, a fisherman's net.

Franco was moving more slowly now. He was fighting a kid – nothing more. The little brat might have surprised him with that first attack, but it would be easy enough to bring this to an end.

He muttered a few words in French: something low and ugly. Then, a second later, his fist swung through the air, this time carrying the knife in an upward arc that would have cut Alex's throat if he hadn't thrown himself backwards.

Alex cried out.

He had lost his footing, falling heavily onto his back, one arm outstretched. Franco grinned, showing two gold teeth, and stepped towards him, anxious to finish this off. Too late he saw that he had been tricked. Alex's hand had caught hold of the net. As Franco loomed over him, he sprang up, swinging his arm forward with all his strength. The net spread out, falling over Franco's head, shoulder and knife hand. He swore and twisted round, trying to free himself, but the movement only entangled him all the more.

Alex knew he had to finish this quickly. Franco was still struggling with the net but Alex saw him open his mouth to call for help. They were right next to the yacht. If Yassen heard any-thing, there would be nothing more Alex could do. He took aim and kicked a second time, his foot driving into the man's stomach. The breath was knocked out of him; Alex saw his face turn red. He was half out of the net, performing a bizarre dance on the edge of the jetty, when he lost his balance and fell. With his hands trapped he couldn't protect himself. His head hit the concrete with a loud crack and he lay still.

Alex stood, breathing heavily. In the distance he heard a trumpet blare and there was a scattered round of applause. The bullfight was due to begin in ten minutes. A small band had arrived and was about to play. Alex looked at the unconscious man, knowing he had had a close escape. There was no sign of the knife; maybe it had fallen into the water. Briefly he wondered if he should go on. Then he thought of Sabina and her father, and the next thing he knew he had climbed the gangplank and was standing on the deck.

The boat was called *Fer de Lance*. Alex noticed the name as he climbed up, and remembered seeing it somewhere else. That was it! It was on a school trip to London Zoo. It was some sort of snake. Poisonous, of course.

He was standing in a wide area with a steering wheel and controls next to a door on one side and leather sofas across the back. There was a low table. The bald man must have been sitting here before he went down for his smoke. Alex saw a crumpled magazine, a bottle of beer, a mobile phone and a gun.

He recognized the telephone. It was Yassen's. He had seen it in the Russian's hand back at the restaurant earlier that day. The phone was an odd colour – a shade of brown – otherwise Alex might have ignored it. But now he noticed that it was still turned on. He picked it up.

Alex quickly scrolled to the main menu and then to Call Register. He found what he was looking for: a record of all the calls Yassen had received that day. At 12.53 he had been talking to a number that began 44207. The 44 was England; the 207 meant it was somewhere in London. That was the call Alex had overheard in the restaurant. Quickly he memorized the number. It was the number of the person who had given Yassen his orders. It would tell him all he needed to know.

He picked up the gun.

He finally had it. Each time he had worked for MI6 he had asked them to give him a gun, and each time they had refused. They had supplied him with gadgets – but only tranquillizer darts, stun grenades, smoke bombs. Nothing that would kill. Alex felt the power of the weapon he was holding. He weighed it in his hand. The gun was a Grach MP-443, black, with a short muzzle and a ribbed stock. It was Russian, of course, new army issue. He allowed his finger to curl around the trigger and smiled grimly. Now he and Yassen were equals.

He padded forward, went through the door and climbed down a short flight of stairs that went below deck and into a corridor that seemed to run the length of the boat, with cabins on either side. He had seen a lounge above but he knew that it was empty. There had been no lights behind those windows. If Yassen was anywhere, he would be down here. Clutching the Grach more tightly, he crept along, his feet making no sound on the thickly carpeted floor.

He came to a door and saw a yellow strip of light seeping out of the crack below. Gritting his teeth, he reached for the handle, half hoping it would be locked. The handle turned and the door opened. Alex went in.

The cabin was surprisingly large, a long rectangle with a white carpet and modern wooden fittings along two of the walls. The third wall was taken up by a low double bed with a table and a lamp on each side. There was a man stretched out on the white cover, his eyes closed, as still as a corpse. Alex stepped forward. There was no sound in the room, but in the distance he could hear the band playing at the bullring: two or three trumpets, a tuba and a drum.

Yassen Gregorovich made no movement as Alex approached, the gun held out in front of him. Alex reached the side of the bed. This was the closest he had ever been to the Russian, the man who had killed his uncle. He could see every detail of his face: the chiselled lips, the almost feminine eyelashes. The gun was only a centimetre from Yassen's forehead. This was where it ended. All he had to do was pull the trigger and it would be over.

"Good evening, Alex."

It wasn't that Yassen had woken up. His eyes had been closed and now they weren't. It was as simple as that. His face hadn't changed. He knew who Alex was immediately, at the same time taking in the gun that was pointing at him. Taking it in and accepting it.

Alex said nothing. There was a slight tremble in the hand holding the gun and he brought his other hand up to steady it.

"You have my gun," Yassen said.

Alex took a breath.

"Do you intend to use it?"

Nothing.

Yassen continued calmly. "I think you should consider very carefully. Killing a man is not like you see on the television. If you pull that trigger, you will fire a real bullet into real flesh and blood. I will feel nothing; I will be dead instantly. But you will live with what you have done for the rest of your life. You will never forget it."

He paused, letting his words hang in the air.

"Do you really have it in you, Alex? Can you make your finger obey you? Can you kill me?"

Alex was rigid, a statue. All his concentration was focused on the finger curled around the trigger. It was simple. There was a spring mechanism. The trigger would pull back the hammer and release it. The hammer would strike the bullet, a piece of death just nineteen millimetres long, sending it on its short, fast journey into this man's head. He could do it.

"Maybe you have forgotten what I once told you. This isn't your life. This has nothing to do with you."

Yassen was totally relaxed. There was no emotion in his voice. He seemed to know Alex better than Alex knew himself. Alex tried to look away, to avoid the calm blue eyes that were watching him with something like pity.

"Why did you do it?" Alex demanded. "You blew up the house. Why?"

The eyes flickered briefly. "Because I was paid."

"Paid to kill me?"

"No, Alex." For a moment Yassen sounded almost amused. "It had nothing to do with you."

"Then who—"

But it was too late.

He saw it in Yassen's eyes first, knew that the Russian had been keeping him distracted as the cabin door opened quietly behind him. A pair of hands seized him and he was swung violently away from the bed. He saw Yassen whip aside as fast as a snake – as fast as a fer de lance. The gun went off, but Alex hadn't fired it intentionally and the bullet smashed into the floor. He hit a wall and felt the gun drop out of his hand. He could taste blood in his mouth. The yacht seemed to be swaying.

In the far distance a fanfare sounded, followed by an echoing roar from the crowd. The bullfight had begun.

MATADOR

Alex sat listening to the three men who would decide his fate, trying to understand what they were saying. They were speaking French, but with an almost impenetrable Marseilles accent – and they were using gutter language, not the sort he had learnt.

He had been dragged up to the main saloon and was slumped in a wide leather armchair. By now Alex had managed to work out what had happened. The deckhand, Raoul, had come back from the town with supplies and found Franco lying unconscious on the jetty. He had hurried on board to alert Yassen and had overheard him talking to Alex. It had been Raoul, of course, who had crept into the cabin and grabbed Alex from behind.

Franco was sitting in a corner, his face distorted with anger and hatred. There was a dark mauve bruise on his forehead where he had hit the ground. When he spoke, his words dripped poison.

"Give me the little brat. I will kill him personally and then drop him over the side for the fish."

"How did he find us, Yassen?" This was Raoul speaking. "How did he know who we are?"

"Why are we wasting our time with him? Let me finish him now."

Alex glanced at Yassen. So far the Russian had said nothing, although it was clear he was still in charge. There was something curious about the way he was looking at Alex. The empty blue eyes gave nothing away and yet Alex felt he was being appraised. It was as if Yassen had known him a long time and had expected to meet him again.

Yassen lifted a hand for silence, then went over to Alex. "How did you know you would find us here?" he asked.

Alex said nothing. A flicker of annoyance passed across the Russian's face. "You are only alive because I permit it. Please don't make me ask you a second time."

Alex shrugged. He had nothing to lose. They

were probably going to kill him anyway. "I was on holiday," he said. "I was on the beach. I saw you on the yacht when it came in."

"You are not with MI6?"

"No."

"But you followed me to the restaurant."

"That's right." Alex nodded.

Yassen half smiled to himself. "I thought there was someone." Then he was serious again. "You were staying in the house."

"I was invited by a friend," Alex said. A thought suddenly occurred to him. "Her dad's a journalist. Was he the one you wanted to kill?"

"That is none of your business."

"It is now."

"It was bad luck you were staying with him, Alex. I've already told you. It was nothing personal."

"Sure." Alex looked Yassen straight in the eye. "With you it never is."

Yassen went back over to the two men and at once Franco began to jabber again, spitting out his words. He had poured himself a whisky which he downed in a single swallow, his eyes never leaving Alex.

"The boy knows nothing and he can't hurt us," Yassen said. He was speaking in English – for his benefit, Alex guessed.

"What you do with him?" Raoul asked, following in clumsy English too.

"Kill him!" This was Franco.

"I do not kill children," Yassen replied, and Alex knew that he was telling only half the truth. The bomb in the house could have killed anyone who happened to be there and Yassen wouldn't have cared.

"Have you gone mad?" Franco had slipped back into French. "You can't just let him walk away from here. He came to kill you. If it hadn't been for Raoul, he might have succeeded."

"Maybe." Yassen studied Alex one last time. Finally he came to a decision. "You were unwise to come here, little Alex," he said. "These people think I should silence you and they are right. If I thought it was anything but chance that brought you to me, if there was anything that you knew, you would already be dead. But I am a reasonable man. You did not kill me when you had the chance, so now I will give you a chance too."

He spoke rapidly to Franco in French. At first Franco seemed sullen, argumentative. But as Yassen continued, Alex saw a smile spread slowly across his face.

"How will we arrange this?" Franco asked.

"You know people. You have influence. You just have to pay the right people."

"The boy will be killed."

"Then you will have your wish."

"Good!" Franco spat. "I'll enjoy watching!"

Yassen came over to Alex and stopped just a short distance away. "You have courage, Alex," he said. "I admire that in you. Now I am going to give you the opportunity to display it." He nodded at Franco. "Take him!"

It was nine o'clock. The night had rolled in over Saint-Pierre, bringing with it the threat of a summer storm. The air was still and heavy and thick cloud had blotted out the stars.

Alex stood on sandy ground in the shadows of a concrete archway, unable to take in what was happening to him. He had been forced, at gunpoint, to change his holiday clothes for a uniform so bizarre that, but for his knowledge of the danger he was about to face, he would have felt simply ridiculous.

First there had been a white shirt and a black tie. Then came a jacket with shoulder pads hanging over his arms and a pair of trousers that fitted tight around his thighs and waist but stopped well short of his ankles. Both of these were covered in gold sequins and thousands of tiny pearls, so that as Alex moved in and out of the light he became a miniature fireworks display. Finally he had been given black shoes, an odd, curving black hat, and a bright red cape which was folded over his arm.

The uniform had a name. *Traje de luces*. The suit of lights worn by matadors in the bullring. This was the test of courage that Yassen had somehow arranged. He wanted Alex to fight a bull.

Now he stood next to Alex, listening to the noise of the crowd inside the arena. At a typical bullfight, he had explained, six bulls are killed. The third of these is sometimes taken by the least experienced matador, a *novillero*, a young man who might be in the ring for the first time. There had been no *novillero* on the programme tonight ... not until the Russian had suggested otherwise. Money had changed hands. And Alex had been prepared. It was insane – but the crowd would love him. Once he was inside the arena, nobody would know that he had never been trained. He would be a tiny figure in the middle of the floodlit ring. His clothes would disguise the truth. Nobody would see that he was only fourteen.

There was an eruption of shouting and cheering inside the arena. Alex guessed that the matador had just killed the second bull.

"Why are you doing this?" Alex asked.

Yassen shrugged. "I'm doing you a favour, Alex."

"I don't see it that way."

"Franco wanted to put a knife in you. It was hard to dissuade him. In the end I offered him a little entertainment. As it happens, he greatly admires this sport. This way he gets amused and you get a choice."

"A choice?"

"You might say it is a choice between the bull and the bullet."

"Either way I get killed."

"Yes. That is the most likely outcome, I'm afraid. But at least you will have a heroic death. A thousand people will be watching you. Their voices will be the last thing you hear."

"Better than hearing yours," Alex growled.

And suddenly it was time.

Two men in jeans and black shirts ran forward and opened a gate. It was like a wooden curtain being drawn across a stage and it revealed a fantastic scene behind. First there was the arena itself, an elongated circle of bright yellow sand.

As Yassen had promised, it was surrounded by a thousand people, tightly packed in tiers. They were eating and drinking, many of them waving programmes in front of their faces, trying to shift the sluggish air, jostling and talking. Although all of them were seated, none of them were still. In the far corner a band played, five men in military uniforms, looking like antique toys. The glare from the spotlights was dazzling.

Empty, the arena was modern, ugly and dead. But filled to the brim on this hot Mediterranean night, Alex could feel the energy buzzing through it, and he realized that all the cruelty of the Romans with their gladiators and wild animals had survived the centuries and was fully alive here.

A tractor drove towards the gate where Alex was standing, dragging behind it a misshapen black lump that had until seconds ago been a proud and living thing. About a dozen brightly coloured spears dangled out of the creature's back. As it drew nearer, Alex saw that it was leaving a comma of glistening red in the sand. He felt sick, and wondered if it was fear of what was to come or disgust and hatred of what had been. He and Sabina had agreed that they would never in a million years go to a bullfight. He certainly hadn't expected to break that promise so soon.

Yassen nodded at him. "Remember," he said, "Raoul, Franco and I will be beside the *barrera* – that's right at the side of the ring. If you fail to perform, if you try to run, we will gun you down and disappear into the night." He raised his shirt to show Alex the Grach, tucked into his waistband. "But if you agree to fight, after ten minutes we will leave. If by some miracle you are still standing, you can do as you please. You see? I am giving you a chance."

The trumpets sounded again, announcing the next fight. Alex felt a hand press into the small of his back and he walked forward, giddy with disbelief. How had this been allowed to happen? Surely someone would see that underneath the fancy dress he was just an English schoolboy, not a matador or a *novillero* or whatever it was called. Someone would have to stop the fight.

But the spectators were already shouting their approval. A few flowers rained down in his direction. Nobody could see the truth and Franco had paid enough money to make sure they didn't find out until it was too late. He had to go through with this. His heart was thumping. The smell of blood and animal sweat rose in his nostrils. He was more afraid than he had ever been.

A man in an elaborate black silk suit with mother-of-pearl buttons and sweeping shoulders stood up in the crowd and raised a white handkerchief. This was the president of the bullring, giving the signal for the next fight. The trumpets sounded. Another gate opened and the bull that Alex was to fight thundered into the ring like a bullet fired from a gun. Alex stared. The creature was huge – a mass of black, shimmering muscle. It must have weighed seven or eight hundred kilograms. If it ran into him, it would be like being run over by a bus – except that he would be impaled first on the horns that corkscrewed out of its head, tapering to two lethal points. Right now it was ignoring Alex, running madly in a jagged circle, kicking out with its back legs, enraged by the lights and the shouting crowd.

Alex wondered why he hadn't been given a sword. Didn't matadors have anything to defend themselves with? There was a spear lying on the sand, left over from the last fight. This was a *banderilla*. It was about a metre long with a decorated, multicoloured handle and a short, barbed hook. Dozens of these would be plunged into the bull's neck, destroying its muscles and weakening it before the final kill. Alex himself would be given a spear as the fight continued, but he had already made a decision. Whatever happened, he would try not to hurt the bull. After all, it hadn't chosen to be here either.

He had to escape. The gates had been closed but the wooden wall enclosing the arena – the *barrera*, as Yassen had called it – was no taller than he was. He could run and jump over it. He glanced at the wall where he had just come in. Franco had taken his place in the front row. His hand was underneath his jacket and Alex had no doubt what it was holding. He could make out Yassen at the far end. Raoul was over to his right. Between them the three men had the whole ring covered.

He had to fight. Somehow he had to survive ten minutes. Maybe there were only nine minutes now. It felt as if an eternity had passed since he had entered the ring.

The crowd fell silent. A thousand faces waited for him to make his move.

Then the bull noticed him.

Suddenly it stopped its circling and lumbered towards him, coming to a halt about twenty metres away, its head low and its horns pointing at him. Alex knew with a sick certainty that it was about to charge. Reluctantly he allowed the red cape to drop so that it hung down to the sand.

God – he must look an idiot in this costume, with no idea what he was meant to be doing. He was surprised the fight hadn't been stopped already. But Yassen and the two men would be watching his every move. Franco would need only the smallest excuse to draw his gun. Alex had to play his part.

Silence. The heat of the coming storm pressed down on him. Nothing moved.

The bull charged. Alex was shocked by the sudden transformation. The bull had been static and distant. Now it was bearing down on him as if a switch had been thrown, its massive shoulders heaving, its every muscle concentrated on the target that stood waiting, unarmed, alone. The animal was near enough now for Alex to be able to see its eyes: black, white and red, bloodshot and furious.

Everything happened very quickly. The bull was almost on top of him. The vicious horns were plunging towards his stomach. The stench of the animal smothered him. Alex leapt aside, at the same time lifting the cape, imitating moves he had seen ... perhaps on television or in the cinema. He actually felt the bull brush past, and in that tiny contact sensed its huge power and strength. There was a flash of red as the cape flew up. The whole arena seemed to spin, the crowd rising up and yelling. The bull had gone past. Alex was unhurt.

Although he didn't know it, Alex had executed a reasonable imitation of the *verónica*. This is the first and most simple movement in a bullfight, but it gives the matador vital information about his opponent: its speed, its strength, which horn it favours. But Alex had learnt only two things. Matadors were braver than he thought – insanely brave to do this out of choice! And he also knew he was going to be very lucky to survive a second attack.

The bull had stopped at the far end of the ring. It shook its head, and grey strings of saliva whipped from either side of its mouth. All around, the spectators were still clapping. Alex saw Yassen Gregorovich sitting among them. He alone was still, not joining in the applause. Grimly, Alex let the cape hang down a second time, wondering how many minutes had passed. He no longer had any sense of time.

He actually felt the crowd catch its breath as the bull began its second attack. It was moving even faster this time, its hooves pounding on the sand. The horns were once again levelled at him. If they hit him, they would cut him in half.

At the very last moment, Alex stepped aside, repeating the movement he had made before. But this time the bull had been expecting it. Although it was advancing too fast to change direction, it flicked its head and Alex felt a searing pain along the side of his stomach. He was thrown off his feet, cartwheeling backwards and crashing down onto the sand. A roar exploded from the crowd. Alex waited for the bull to turn round and lay into him. But he had been lucky. The animal hadn't seen him go down. It had continued its run to the other side of the arena, leaving him alone.

Alex got to his feet. He put a hand down to his stomach. The jacket had been ripped open and when he took his hand away there was bright red blood on his palm. He was winded and shaken, and the side of his body felt as if it were on fire. But the cut wasn't too deep. In a way, Alex was disappointed. If he had been more badly hurt, they would have had to stop the fight.

Out of the corner of his eye he saw a movement. Yassen had stood up and was walking out. Had the ten minutes passed or had the Russian decided that the entertainment was over and that there was no point staying to watch the bloody end? Alex checked around the arena.

Raoul was leaving too. But Franco was staying in his seat. The man was in the front row, only about ten metres away. And he was smiling. Yassen had tricked him. Franco was going to stay there. Even if Alex did manage to escape the bull, Franco would take out his gun and finish it himself.

Weakly Alex leant down and picked up the cape. The material had got torn in the last encounter and it gave Alex a sudden idea. Everything was in its right place: the cape, the bull, the single *banderilla*, Franco.

Ignoring the pain in his side, he started to run. The audience muttered and then roared in disbelief. It was the bull's job to attack the matador, but suddenly, in front of them, it seemed to be happening the other way round. Even the bull was taken unawares, regarding Alex as if he had forgotten the rules of the game or decided to cheat. Before it had a chance to move, Alex threw the cape. There was a short wooden handle sewn into the cloth and the weight of it carried the whole thing forward so that it landed perfectly – over the creature's eyes. The bull tried to shake the cloth free, but one of its horns had passed through the hole. It snorted angrily and stamped at the ground. But the cape stayed in place.

Everyone was shouting now. Half the spectators

had risen to their feet and the president was looking around him helplessly. Alex ran and snatched up the *banderilla*, noticing the ugly hook, stained red with the blood of the last bull. In a single movement he swung it round and threw it.

His target wasn't the bull. Franco had started to rise out of his seat as soon as he'd realized what Alex was about to do; his hand was already scrabbling for his gun. But he was too late. Either Alex had been lucky or sheer desperation had perfected his aim. The *banderilla* turned once in the air, then buried itself in Franco's shoulder. Franco screamed. The point wasn't long enough to kill him, but the barbed hook kept the *banderilla* in place, making it impossible to pull out. Blood spread along the sleeve of his suit.

The whole arena was in an uproar. The crowd had never seen anything like this. Alex continued running. He saw the bull free itself from the red cape. It was already searching for him, determined to take its revenge.

Take your revenge another day, Alex thought. I have no quarrel with you.

He had reached the *barrera* and leapt up, grabbed the top and pulled himself over. Franco was too shocked and in too much pain to react;

anyway, he had been surrounded by onlookers trying to help. He would never have been able to produce his gun and take aim. Everybody seemed to be on the edge of panic. The president signalled furiously and the band struck up again, but the musicians all began at different times and none of them played the same tune.

One of the men in jeans and black shirts sprinted towards Alex, shouting something in French. Alex ignored him. He hit the ground and ran.

At the very moment that Alex shot out into the night, the storm broke. The rain fell like an ocean thrown from the sky. It crashed into the town, splattered off the pavements and formed instant rivers that raced along the gutters and overwhelmed the drains. There was no thunder. Just this avalanche of water that threatened to drown the world.

Alex didn't stop. In seconds his hair was soaked. Water ran in rivulets down his face and he could barely see. As he ran he tore off the outer parts of the matador's costume, first the hat, then the jacket and tie, throwing each item away, leaving their memory behind.

The sea was on his left, the water black and boiling as it was hit by the rain. Alex twisted off the road and felt sand beneath his feet. He was on the beach – the same beach where he had been lying with Sabina when all this began. The sea wall and the jetty were beyond it.

He leapt onto the sea wall and climbed the heavy boulders. His shirt hung out of his trousers; it was already sodden, clinging to his chest.

Yassen's boat had left.

Alex couldn't be sure, but he thought he could see a vague shape disappearing into the darkness and the rain and he knew that he must have missed it by seconds. He stopped, panting. What had he been thinking of anyway? If the *Fer de Lance* had still been there, would he really have climbed aboard a second time? Of course not. He had been lucky to survive the first attempt. He had come here just in time to see it leave and he had learnt nothing.

No.

There was something.

Alex stood there for a few more moments with the rain streaming down his face, then turned and walked back into the town.

He found the phone box in a street just behind the main church. He had no money so was forced to make a reverse charge call and he wondered if it would be accepted. He dialled the operator and gave the number that he had found and memorized in Yassen's mobile phone.

"Who is speaking?" the operator asked.

Alex hesitated. Then... "My name is Yassen Gregorovich," he said.

There was a long silence as the connection was made. Would anyone even answer? England was an hour behind France but it was still late at night.

The rain was falling more lightly now, pattering on the glass roof of the phone box. Alex waited. Then the operator came back on.

"Your call has been accepted, monsieur. Please go ahead..."

More silence. Then a voice. It spoke just two words.

"Damian Cray."

Alex said nothing.

The voice spoke again. "Hello? Who is this?"

Alex was shivering. Maybe it was the rain; maybe it was a reaction to everything that had happened. He couldn't speak. He heard the man breathing at the end of the line.

Then there was a click and the phone went dead.

TRUTH AND CONSEQUENCE

London greeted Alex like an old and reliable friend. Red buses, black cabs, blue-uniformed policemen and grey clouds ... could he be any-where else? Walking down the King's Road, he felt a million miles from the Camargue – not just home, but back in the real world. The side of his stomach was still sore and he could feel the pressure of the bandage against his skin, but otherwise Yassen and the bullfight were already slipping into the distant past.

He stopped outside a bookshop which, like so many of them, advertised itself with the wafting smell of coffee. He paused for a moment, then went in.

He quickly found what he was looking for. There were three books on Damian Cray in the biography section. Two of these were hardly books at all – more glossy brochures put out by record companies to promote the man who had made them so many millions. The first was called *Damian Cray – Live!* It was stacked next to a book called *Cray-zee! The Life and Times of Damian Cray*. The same face stared out from the covers. Jet-black hair cut short like a schoolboy's. A very round face with prominent cheeks and brilliant green eyes. A small nose, almost too exactly placed right in the middle. Thick lips and perfect white teeth.

The third book had been written quite a few years later. The face was a little older, the eyes hidden behind blue-tinted spectacles, and this Damian Cray was climbing out of a white Rolls-Royce, wearing a Versace suit and tie. The title of the book showed what else had changed: *Sir Damian Cray: The Man, The Music, The Millions*. Alex glanced at the first page, but the heavy, complicated prose soon put him off. It seemed to have been written by someone who probably read the *Financial Times* for laughs.

In the end he didn't buy any of the books. He wanted to know more about Cray, but he didn't think these books would tell him anything he didn't know already. And certainly not why Cray's private telephone number had been on the mobile phone of a hired assassin.

Alex walked back through Chelsea, turning off down the pretty, white-fronted street where his uncle, Ian Rider, had lived. He now shared the house with Jack Starbright, an American girl who had once been the housekeeper but had since become his legal guardian and closest friend. She was the reason Alex had first agreed to work for MI6. He had been sent undercover to spy on Herod Sayle and his Stormbreaker computers. In return she had been given a visa which allowed her to stay in London and look after him.

She was waiting for him in the kitchen when he got in. He had agreed to be back by one and she had thrown together a quick lunch. Jack was a good cook but refused to make anything that took longer than ten minutes. She was twenty-eight years old, slim, with tangled red hair and the sort of face that couldn't help being cheerful, even when she was in a bad mood.

"Had a good morning?" she asked as he came in.

"Yes." Alex sat down slowly, holding his side.

Jack noticed but said nothing. "I hope you're hungry," she went on.

"What's for lunch?"

"Stir-fry."

"It smells good."

"It's an old Chinese recipe. At least, that's what it said on the packet. Help yourself to some Coke and I'll serve up."

The food was good and Alex tried to eat, but the truth was that he had no appetite and he soon gave up. Jack said nothing as he carried his half-finished plate over to the sink, but then she suddenly turned round.

"Alex, you can't keep blaming yourself for what happened in France."

Alex had been about to leave the kitchen but now he returned to the table.

"It's about time you and I talked about this," Jack went on. "In fact, it's time we talked about everything!" She pushed her own plate of food away and waited until Alex had sat down. "All right. So it turns out that your uncle – Ian – wasn't a bank manager. He was a spy. Well, it would have been nice if he'd mentioned it to me, but it's too late now because he's gone and got himself killed, which leaves me stuck here, looking after you." She quickly held up a hand. "I didn't mean that. I love being here. I love London. I even love you.

"But *you're* not a spy, Alex. You know that. Even if Ian had some crazy idea about training you up. Three times now you've taken time off from school and each time you've come back a bit more bashed around. I don't even want to know what you've been up to, but personally I've been worried sick!"

"It wasn't my choice..." Alex said.

"That's my point exactly. Spies and bullets and madmen who want to take over the world – it's got nothing to do with you. So you were right to walk away in Saint-Pierre. You did the right thing."

Alex shook his head. "I should have done something. Anything. If I had, Sabina's dad would never—"

"You can't know that. Even if you'd called the cops, what could they have done? Remember – nobody knew there was a bomb. Nobody knew who the target was. I don't think it would have made any difference at all. And if you don't mind my saying so, Alex, going after this guy Yassen on your own was frankly ... well, it was very dangerous. You're lucky you weren't killed."

She was certainly right about that. Alex remembered the arena and saw again the horns and bloodshot eyes of the bull. He reached out for his glass and took a sip of Coke. "I still have to do something," he said. "Edward Pleasure was writing an article about Damian Cray. Something about a secret meeting in Paris. Maybe he was buying drugs or something."

But even as he spoke the words, Alex knew they couldn't be true. Cray hated drugs. There had been advertising campaigns – posters and TV – using his name and face. His last album, *White Lines*, had contained four anti-drugs songs. He had made it a personal issue. "Maybe he's into porn," he suggested weakly.

"Whatever it is, it's going to be hard to prove, Alex. The whole world loves Damian Cray." Jack sighed. "Maybe you should talk to Mrs Jones."

Alex felt his heart sink. He dreaded the thought of going back to MI6 and meeting the woman who was its deputy head of Special Operations. But he knew Jack was right. At least Mrs Jones would be able to investigate. "I suppose I could go and see her," he said.

"Good. But just make sure she doesn't get you involved. If Damian Cray *is* up to something, it's her business – not yours."

The telephone rang.

There was a cordless phone in the kitchen and Jack took the call. She listened for a moment, then handed the receiver to Alex. "It's Sabina," she said. "For you."

* * *

They met outside Tower Records in Piccadilly
Circus and walked to a nearby Starbucks. Sabina
was wearing grey trousers and a loose-fitting
jersey. Alex had expected her to have changed in
some way after all that had happened, and indeed
she looked younger, less sure of herself. She was
obviously tired. All traces of her South of France
suntan had disappeared.

"Dad's going to live," she said as they sat down
together with two bottles of juice. "The doctors
are pretty sure about that. He's strong and he
kept himself fit. But..." Her voice trembled. "It's
going to take a long time, Alex. He's still unconscious – and he was badly burnt." She stopped
and drank some of her juice. "The police said it
was a gas leak. Can you believe that? Mum says
she's going to sue."

"Who's she going to sue?"

"The people who rented us the house. The gas
board. The whole country. She's furious..."

Alex said nothing. A gas leak. That was what
the police had told him.

Sabina sighed. "Mum said I ought to see you.
She said you'd want to know about Dad."

"Your dad had just come down from Paris,
hadn't he?" Alex wasn't sure this was the right

time, but he had to know. "Did he say anything about the article he was writing?"

Sabina looked surprised. "No. He never talked about his work. Not to Mum. Not to anyone."

"Where had he been?"

"He'd been staying with a friend. A photographer."

"Do you know his name?"

"Marc Antonio. Why are you asking all these questions about my dad? Why do you want to know?"

Alex avoided the questions. "Where is he now?" he asked.

"In hospital in France. He's not strong enough to travel. Mum's still out there with him. I flew home on my own."

Alex thought for a moment. This wasn't a good idea. But he couldn't keep silent. Not knowing what he did. "I think he should have a police guard," he said.

"What?" Sabina stared at him. "Why? Are you saying ... it wasn't a gas leak?"

Alex didn't answer.

Sabina looked at him carefully, then came to a decision. "You've been asking a lot of questions," she said. "Now it's my turn. I don't know what's really going on, but Mum told me that after it happened, you ran away from the house."

"How did she know?"

"The police told her. They said you had this idea that someone had tried to kill Dad ... and that it was someone you knew. And then you disappeared. They were searching everywhere for you."

"I went to the police station at Saint-Pierre," Alex said.

"But that wasn't until midnight. You were completely soaked and you had a cut and you were dressed in weird clothes..."

Alex had been questioned for an hour when he had finally shown up at the gendarmerie. A doctor had given him three stitches and bandaged up the wound. Then a policeman had brought him a change of clothes. The questions had only stopped with the arrival of the man from the British consulate in Lyons. The man, who had been elderly and efficient, seemed to know all about Alex. He had driven Alex to Montpellier Airport to catch the first flight the next day. He had no interest in what had happened. His only desire seemed to be to get Alex out of the country.

"What were you doing?" Sabina asked. "You say Dad needs protection. Is there something you know?"

"I can't really tell you—" Alex began.

"Stuff that!" Sabina said. "Of course you can tell me!"

"I can't. You wouldn't believe me."

"If you don't tell me, Alex, I'm going to walk out of here and you'll never see me again. What is it that you know about my dad?"

In the end he told her. It was very simple. She hadn't given him any choice. And in a way he was glad. The secret had been with him too long and carrying it alone, he had begun to feel it weighing him down.

He began with the death of his uncle, his introduction to MI6, his training and his first meeting with Yassen Gregorovich at the Stormbreaker computer plant in Cornwall. He described, as briefly as he could, how he had been forced, twice more, to work for MI6 – in the French Alps and off the coast of America. Then he told her what he had felt the moment he had seen Yassen on the beach at Saint-Pierre, how he had followed him to the restaurant, why in the end he had done nothing.

He thought he had skimmed over it all but in fact he talked for half an hour before arriving at his meeting with Yassen on the *Fer de Lance*. He had avoided looking directly at Sabina for much of the time as he talked, but when he reached the bullfight, describing how he had dressed up as a matador and walked out in front of a crowd of a thousand, he glanced up and met her eyes. She was looking at him as if seeing him for the first time. She almost seemed to hate him.

"I told you it wasn't easy to believe," he concluded lamely.

"Alex..."

"I know the whole thing sounds mad. But that's what happened. I am so sorry about your dad. I'm sorry I couldn't stop it from happening. But at least I know who was responsible."

"Who?"

"Damian Cray."

"The pop star?"

"Your dad was writing an article about him. I found a bit of it at the house. And his number was on Yassen's mobile phone."

"So Damian Cray wanted to kill my dad."

"Yes."

There was a long silence. Too long, Alex thought.

At last Sabina spoke again. "I'm sorry, Alex," she said. "I have never heard so much crap in all my life."

"Sab, I told you—"

"I know you said I wouldn't believe it. But just because you said that, it doesn't make it true!" She shook her head. "How can you expect anyone to believe a story like that? Why can't you tell me the truth?"

"It *is* the truth, Sab."

Suddenly he knew what he had to do.

"And I can prove it."

They took the tube across London to Liverpool Street Station and walked up the road to the building that Alex knew housed the Special Operations division of MI6. They found themselves standing in front of a tall, black-painted door, the sort that was designed to impress people coming in or leaving. Next to it, screwed into the brickwork, was a brass plaque with the words:

> **ROYAL & GENERAL BANK PLC**
>
> **LONDON**

Sabina had seen it. She looked at Alex doubtfully.

"Don't worry," Alex said. "The Royal & General Bank doesn't exist. That's just the sign they put on the door."

They went in. The entrance hall was cold and businesslike, with high ceilings and a brown marble floor. To one side there was a leather sofa and Alex remembered sitting there the first time he had come, waiting to go up to his uncle's office on the fifteenth floor. He walked straight across to the glass reception desk where a young woman was sitting with a microphone curving across her mouth, taking calls and greeting visitors at the same time. There was an older security officer in uniform and peaked cap next to her.

"Can I help you?" the woman asked, smiling at Alex and Sabina.

"Yes," Alex said. "I'd like to see Mrs Jones."

"Mrs Jones?" The young woman frowned. "Do you know what department she works in?"

"She works with Mr Blunt."

"I'm sorry..." She turned to the security guard. "Do you know a Mrs Jones?"

"There's a Miss Johnson," the guard suggested. "She's a cashier."

Alex looked from one to the other. "You know who I mean," he said. "Just tell her that Alex Rider is here—"

"There is no Mrs Jones working at this bank," the receptionist interrupted.

"Alex..." Sabina began.

But Alex refused to give up. He leant forward so that he could speak confidentially. "I know this isn't a bank," he said. "This is MI6 Special Operations. Please could you—"

"Are you doing this as some sort of prank?" This time it was the security guard who was speaking. "What's all this nonsense about MI6?"

"Alex, let's get out of here," Sabina said.

"No!" Alex couldn't believe what was happening. He didn't even know exactly what it *was* that was happening. It had to be a mistake. These people were new. Or perhaps they needed some sort of password to allow him into the building. Of course. On his previous visits here, he had only ever come when he had been expected. Either that or he had been brought here against his will. This time he had come unannounced. That was why he wasn't being allowed in.

"Listen," Alex said. "I understand why you wouldn't want to let just anyone in, but I'm not just anyone. I'm Alex Rider. I work with Mr Blunt and Mrs Jones. Could you please let her know I'm here?"

"There *is* no Mrs Jones," the receptionist repeated helplessly.

"And I don't know any Mr Blunt either," the security guard added.

"Alex. Please..." Sabina was sounding more and more desperate. She really wanted to leave.

Alex turned to her. "They're lying, Sabina," he said. "I'll show you."

He grabbed her arm and pulled her over to the lift. He reached out and stabbed the call button.

"You stop right there!" The security guard stood up.

The receptionist reached out and pressed a button, presumably calling for help.

The lift didn't come.

Alex saw the guard moving towards him. Still no lift. He looked around and noticed a corridor leading away, with a set of swing doors at the end. Perhaps there would be a staircase or another set of lifts somewhere else in the building. Pulling Sabina behind him, Alex set off down the corridor. He heard the security guard getting closer. He quickened his pace, searching for a way up.

He slammed through the double doors.

And stopped.

He was in a banking hall. It was huge, with a domed ceiling and advertisements on the walls for mortgages, savings schemes and personal loans. There were seven or eight glass windows arranged along one side, with cashiers stamping documents and cashing cheques, while about a dozen customers – ordinary people off the street – waited in line. Two personal advisers, young men in smart suits, sat behind desks in the open-plan area. One of them was discussing pension schemes with an elderly couple. Alex heard the other answer his phone.

"Hello. This is the Royal & General Bank, Liverpool Street. Adam speaking. How may I help?"

A light flashed on above one of the windows. Number four. A man in a pinstripe suit went over to it and the queue shuffled forward.

Alex took all this in with one glance. He looked at Sabina. She was staring with a mixture of emotions on her face.

And then the security guard was there. "You're not meant to come into the bank this way," he said. "This is a staff entrance. Now, I want you to leave before you get yourself into real trouble. I mean it! I don't want to have to call the police, but that's my job."

"We're going." Sabina had stepped in and her voice was cold, definite.

"Sab—"

"We're going now."

"You ought to look after your friend," the security guard said. "He may think this sort of thing is funny, but it isn't."

Alex left – or rather allowed Sabina to lead him out. They went through a revolving door and out onto the street. Alex wondered what had happened. Why had he never seen the bank before? Then he realized. The building was actually sandwiched between two streets with a quite separate front and back. He had always entered from the other side.

"Listen—" he began.

"No. You listen! I don't know what's going on inside your head. Maybe it's because you don't have parents. You have to draw attention to yourself by creating this ... fantasy! But just listen to yourself, Alex! I mean, it's pretty sick. Schoolboy spies and Russian assassins and all the rest of it..."

"It's got nothing to do with my parents," Alex said, feeling anger well up inside him.

"But it's got *everything* to do with mine. My dad gets hurt in an accident—"

"It wasn't an accident, Sab." He couldn't stop himself. "Are you really so stupid that you think I'd make all this up?"

"Stupid? Are you calling me stupid?"

"I'm just saying that I thought we were friends. I thought you knew me..."

"Yes! I thought I knew you. But now I see I was wrong. I'll tell you what's stupid. Listening to you in the first place was stupid. Coming to see you was stupid. Ever getting to know you ... that was the most stupid thing of all."

She turned and walked away in the direction of the station. In seconds she had gone, disappearing into the crowd.

"Alex..." a voice said behind him. It was a voice that he knew.

Mrs Jones was standing on the pavement. She had seen and heard everything that had taken place.

"Let her go," she said. "I think we need to talk."

SAINT OR SINGER?

The office was the same as it had always been. The same ordinary, modern furniture, the same view, the same man behind the same desk. Not for the first time, Alex found himself wondering about Alan Blunt, head of MI6 Special Operations. What had his journey to work been like today? Was there a suburban house with a nice, smiling wife and two children waving goodbye as he left to catch the tube? Did his family know the truth about him? Had he ever told them that he wasn't working for a bank or an insurance company or anything like that, and that he carried with him – perhaps in a smart leather case, given to him for his birthday – files and documents full of death?

Alex tried to see the teenager in the man in the grey suit. Blunt must have been his own age once. He would have gone to school, sweated over exams, played football, tried his first cigarette and got bored at weekends like anybody else. But there was no sign of any child in the empty grey eyes, the colourless hair, the mottled, tightly drawn skin. So when had it happened? What had turned him into a civil servant, a spymaster, an adult with no obvious emotions and no remorse?

And then Alex wondered if the same thing would one day happen to him. Was that what MI6 were preparing him for? First they had turned him into a spy; next they would turn him into one of them. Perhaps they already had an office waiting with his name on the door. The windows were closed and it was warm in the room, but he shuddered. He had been wrong to come here with Sabina. The office on Liverpool Street was poisonous, and one way or another it would destroy him if he didn't stay away.

"We couldn't allow you to bring that girl here, Alex," Blunt was saying. "You know perfectly well that you can't just show off to your friends whenever—"

"I wasn't showing off," Alex cut in. "Her dad was almost killed by a bomb in the South of France."

"We know all about the business in Saint-Pierre," Blunt murmured.

"Do you know that it was Yassen Gregorovich who planted it?"

Blunt sighed irritably. "That doesn't make any difference. It's none of your business. And it's certainly nothing to do with us!"

Alex stared at him in disbelief. "Sabina's father is a journalist," he exclaimed. "He was writing about Damian Cray. If Cray wanted him dead, there must be a reason. Isn't it your job to find out?"

Blunt held up a hand for silence. His eyes, as always, showed nothing at all. Alex was struck by the thought that if this man were to die, sitting here at his desk, nobody would notice any difference.

"I have received a report from the police in Montpellier, and also from the British consulate," Blunt said. "This is standard practice when one of our people is involved."

"I'm not one of your people," Alex muttered.

"I am sorry that the father of your ... friend was hurt. But you might as well know that the French police have investigated – and you're right. It wasn't a gas leak."

"That's what I was trying to tell you."

"It turns out that a local terrorist organization – the CST – have claimed responsibility."

"The CST?" Alex's head spun. "Who are they?"

"They're very new," Mrs Jones explained. "CST stands for Camargue Sans Touristes. Essentially they're French nationalists who want to stop local houses in the Camargue being sold off for tourism and second homes."

"It's got nothing to do with the CST," Alex insisted. "It was Yassen Gregorovich. I saw him and he admitted it. And he told me that the real target was Edward Pleasure. Why won't you listen to what I'm saying? It was this article Edward was writing. Something about a meeting in Paris. It was Damian Cray who wanted him dead."

There was a brief pause. Mrs Jones glanced at her boss as if needing his permission to speak. He nodded almost imperceptibly.

"Did Yassen mention Damian Cray?" she asked.

"No. But I found his private telephone number in Yassen's phone. I rang it and I actually heard him speak."

"You can't know it was Damian Cray."

"Well, that was the name he gave."

"This is complete nonsense." It was Blunt who had spoken and Alex was amazed to see that he was angry. It was the first time Alex had ever seen him show any emotion at all and it occurred to him that not many people dared to disagree with the chief executive of Special Operations. Certainly not to his face.

"Why is it nonsense?"

"Because you're talking about one of the most admired and respected entertainers in the country. A man who has raised millions and millions of pounds for charity. Because you're talking about Damian Cray!" Blunt sank back into his chair. For a moment he seemed undecided. Then he nodded briefly. "All right," he said. "Since you have been of some use to us in the past, and since I want to clear this matter up once and for all, I will tell you everything we know about Cray."

"We have extensive files on him," Mrs Jones said.

"Why?"

"We keep extensive files on everyone who's famous."

"Go on."

Blunt nodded again and Mrs Jones took over. She seemed to know all the facts by heart. Either she had read the files recently or, more probably, she had the sort of mind that never forgot anything.

"Damian Cray was born in north London on

5 October 1950," she began. "That's not his real name, by the way. He was christened Harold Eric Lunt. His father was Sir Arthur Lunt, who made his fortune building multi-storey car parks. As a child, Harold had a remarkable singing voice, and aged eleven he was sent to the Royal Academy of Music in London. In fact, he used to sing regularly there with another boy who also became famous. That was Elton John.

"But when he was thirteen, there was a terrible disaster. His parents were killed in a bizarre car accident."

"What was bizarre about it?"

"The car fell on top of them. It rolled off the top floor of one of their car parks. As you can imagine, Harold was distraught. He left the Royal Academy and travelled the world. He changed his name and turned to Buddhism for a while. He also became a vegetarian. Even now, he never touches meat. The tickets for his concerts are made out of recycled paper. He has very strict values and he sticks to them.

"Anyway, he came back to England in the seventies and formed a band – Slam! They were an instant success. I'm sure the rest of this will be very familiar to you, Alex. At the end of the seventies the band split up, and Cray began a solo career which took him to new heights. His first solo album, *Firelight*, went platinum. After that he was seldom out of the UK or US top twenty. He won five Grammys and an Academy Award for Best Original Song. In 1986 he visited Africa and decided to do something to help the people there. He arranged a concert at Wembley Stadium, with all proceeds going to charity. Chart Attack – that was what it was called. It was a huge success and that Christmas he released a single: 'Something for the Children'. It sold four million copies and he gave every penny away.

"That was just the beginning. Since the success of Chart Attack, Cray has campaigned tirelessly on a range of world issues. Save the rainforests; protect the ozone layer; end world debt. He's built his own rehabilitation centres to help young people involved with drugs, and he spent two years fighting to have a laboratory closed down because it was experimenting on animals.

"In 1989 he performed in Belfast, and many people believe that this free concert was a step on the way towards peace in Northern Ireland. A year later he made two visits to Buckingham Palace. He was there on a Thursday to play a solo for Princess Diana's birthday; and on the Friday he was back again to receive a knighthood from the Queen.

"Only last year he was on the cover of *Time* magazine. 'Man of the Year. Saint or Singer?' That was the headline. And that's why your accusations are ridiculous, Alex. The whole world knows that Damian Cray is just about the closest thing we have to a living saint."

"It was still his voice on the telephone," Alex said.

"You heard someone give his name. You don't know it was him."

"I just don't understand it!" Now Alex was angry, confused. "All right, we all like Damian Cray. I know he's famous. But if there's a chance that he was involved with the bomb, why won't you at least investigate him?"

"Because we can't." It was Blunt who had spoken and the words came out flat and heavy. He cleared his throat. "Damian Cray is a multi-millionaire. He's got a huge penthouse on the Thames and another place down in Wiltshire, just outside Bath."

"So what?"

"Rich people have connections and extremely rich people have very good connections indeed. Since the nineties, Cray has been putting his money into a number of commercial ventures. He bought his own television station and made a number of programmes that are now shown all around the world. Then he branched out into hotels – and finally into computer games. He's about to launch a new game system. He calls it the Gameslayer, and apparently it will put all the other systems – PlayStation 2, GameCube, whatever – into the shade."

"I still don't see—"

"He is a major employer, Alex. He is a man of enormous influence. And, for what it's worth, he donated a million pounds to the government just before the last election. Now do you understand? If it was discovered that we were investigating him, and merely on your say-so, there would be a tremendous scandal. The prime minister doesn't like us anyway. He hates anything he can't control. He might even use an attack on Damian Cray as an excuse to close us down."

"Cray was on television only today," Mrs Jones said. She picked up a remote control. "Have a look at this and then tell me what you think."

A TV monitor in the corner of the room flickered on, and Alex found himself looking at a recording of the mid-morning news. He guessed Mrs Jones probably recorded the news every day.

She fast-forwarded, then ran the film at the correct speed.

And there was Damian Cray. His hair was neatly combed and he was wearing a dark, formal suit, white shirt and mauve silk tie. He was standing outside the American embassy in London's Grosvenor Square.

Mrs Jones turned up the sound.

"...the former pop singer, now tireless campaigner for a number of environmental and political issues, Damian Cray. He was in London to meet the president of the United States, who has just arrived in England as part of his summer vacation."

The picture switched to a jumbo jet landing at Heathrow Airport, then cut in closer to show the president standing at the open door, waving and smiling.

"The president arrived at Heathrow Airport in Air Force One, the presidential plane. He is due to have a formal lunch with the prime minister at number ten Downing Street today..."

Another cut. Now the president was standing next to Damian Cray and the two men were shaking hands, a long handshake for the benefit of the cameras which flashed all around them. Cray had sandwiched the president's hand between both his own hands and seemed unwilling to let him go. He said something and the president laughed.

"...but first he met Cray for an informal discussion at the American embassy in London. Cray is a spokesman for Greenpeace and has been leading the movement to prevent oil drilling in the wilds of Alaska, fearing the environmental damage this may cause. Although he made no promises, the president agreed to study the report which Greenpeace..."

Mrs Jones turned off the television.

"Do you see? The most powerful man in the world interrupts his holiday to meet Damian Cray. And he sees Cray before he even visits the prime minister! That should give you the measure of the man. So tell me! What earthly reason could he have to blow up a house and perhaps kill a whole family?"

"That's what I want you to find out."

Blunt sniffed. "I think we should wait for the French police to get back to us," he said. "They're investigating the CST. Let's see what they come up with."

"So you're going to do nothing!"

"I think we have explained, Alex."

"All right." Alex stood up. He didn't try to

conceal his anger. "You've made me look a complete fool in front of Sabina; you've made me lose one of my best friends. It's really amazing. When you need me, you just pull me out of school and send me to the other side of the world. But when I need you, just this once, you pretend you don't even exist and you just dump me out on the street..."

"You're being over-emotional," Blunt said.

"No, I'm not. But I'll tell you this. If you won't go after Cray, I will. He may be Father Christmas, Joan of Arc and the Pope all rolled into one, but it was his voice on the phone and I know he was somehow involved in what happened in the South of France. I'm going to prove it to you."

Alex stood up and, without waiting to hear another word, left the room.

There was a long pause.

Blunt took out a pen and made a few notes on a sheet of paper. Then he looked at Mrs Jones. "Well?" he demanded.

"Maybe we should go over the files one more time," Mrs Jones suggested. "After all, Herod Sayle pretended to be a friend of the British people, and if it hadn't been for Alex..."

"You can do what you like," Blunt said. He drew a ring round the last sentence he had written. Mrs Jones could see the words *Yassen Gregorovich* upside down on the page. "Curious that he should have run into Yassen a second time," he muttered.

"And more curious still that Yassen didn't kill him when he had the chance."

"I wouldn't say that, all things considered."

Mrs Jones nodded. "Maybe we ought to tell Alex about Yassen," she suggested.

"Absolutely not." Blunt picked up the piece of paper and crumpled it. "The less Alex Rider knows about Yassen Gregorovich the better. I very much hope the two of them don't run into each other again." He dropped the paper ball into the bin underneath his desk. At the end of the day everything in the bin would be incinerated.

"And that," he said, "is that."

Jack was worried.

Alex had come back from Liverpool Street in a bleak mood and had barely spoken a word to her since. He had come into the sitting room where she was reading a book and she had managed to learn that the meeting with Sabina hadn't gone well and that Alex wouldn't be seeing her again. But during the afternoon she managed to coax more and more of the story out of him until finally she had the whole picture.

"They're all idiots!" Alex exclaimed. "I know they're wrong but just because I'm younger than them, they won't listen to me."

"I've told you before, Alex. You shouldn't be mixed up with them."

"I won't be. Never again. They don't give a damn about me."

The doorbell rang.

"I'll go," Alex said.

There was a white van parked outside. Two men were opening the back and, as Alex watched, they unloaded a brand-new bicycle, wheeling it down and over to the house. Alex cast his eye over it. The bike was a Cannondale Bad Boy, a mountain bike that had been adapted for the city with a lightweight aluminium frame and one-inch wheels. It was silver and seemed to have come equipped with all the accessories he could have asked for: Digital Evolution lights, a Blackburn mini-pump ... everything top of the range. Only the silver bell on the handlebar seemed old-fashioned and out of place. Alex ran his hand over the leather saddle with its twisting Celtic design and then along the frame, admiring the workman-ship. There was no sign of any welds. The bike was handmade and must have cost hundreds.

One of the men came over to him. "Alex Rider?" he asked.

"Yes. But I think there's been a mistake. I didn't order a bike."

"It's a gift. Here..."

The second man had left the bike propped up against the railings. Alex found himself holding a thick envelope. Jack appeared on the step behind him. "What is it?" she asked.

"Someone has given me a bike."

Alex opened the envelope. Inside was an instruction booklet and attached to it a letter.

Dear Alex,

I'm probably going to get a roasting for this, but I don't like the idea of you taking off on your own without any back-up. This is something I've been working on for you and you might as well have it now. I hope it comes in useful.

Look after yourself, dear boy. I'd hate to hear that anything lethal had happened to you.

All the best,

Smithers

PS This letter will self-destruct ten seconds after it comes into contact with the air so I hope you read it quickly!

Alex just had time to read the last sentence before the letters on the page faded and the paper itself crumpled and turned into white ash. He moved his hands apart and what was left of the letter blew away in the breeze. Meanwhile the two men had got back into the van and driven away. Alex was left with the bike. He flicked through the first pages of the instruction book.

BIKE PUMP – SMOKESCREEN
MAGNESIUM FLARE HEADLAMP
HANDLEBAR MISSILE EJECTION
TRAILRIDER JERSEY (BULLETPROOF)
MAGNETIC BICYCLE CLIPS

"Who is Smithers?" Jack asked. Alex had never told her about him.

"I was wrong," Alex said. "I thought I had no friends at MI6. But it looks like I've got one."

He wheeled the bicycle into the house. Smiling, Jack closed the door.

THE PLEASURE DOME

It was only in the cold light of morning that Alex began to see the impossibility of the task he had set himself. How was he supposed to investigate a man like Cray? Blunt had mentioned that he had homes in London and Wiltshire, but hadn't supplied addresses. Alex didn't even know if Cray was still in England.

But as it turned out, the morning news told Alex where he might begin.

When he came into the kitchen, Jack was reading the newspaper over her second cup of coffee. She took one look at him, then slid it across the table. "This'll put you off your cornflakes."

Alex turned the paper round – and there it was on the second page: Damian Cray looking out at him. A headline ran below the picture:

CRAY LAUNCHES £100M GAMESLAYER

IT'S DEFINITELY THE HOTTEST TICKET IN LONDON. Today game players get to see the eagerly anticipated Gameslayer, developed by Cray Software Technology, a company based in Amsterdam, at a cost rumoured to be in excess of one hundred million pounds. The state-of-the-art game system will be demonstrated by Sir Damian Cray himself in front of an invited audience of journalists, friends, celebrities and industry experts.

No expense has been spared on the launch, which kicks off at one o'clock and includes a lavish champagne buffet inside the Pleasure Dome that Cray has constructed inside Hyde Park. This is the first time that a royal park has been used for a purely commercial venture and there were some critics when permission was given earlier this year.

But Damian Cray is no ordinary businessman. He has already announced that twenty per cent of profits from the Gameslayer will be going to charity, this time helping disabled children throughout the UK. Yesterday Cray met with the United States president to discuss oil drilling in Alaska. It is said that the Queen herself approved the temporary construction of the Pleasure Dome, which uses aluminium and PTFE fabric (the same material used in the Millennium Dome). Its futuristic design has certainly proved an eye-opener for passing Londoners.

Alex stopped reading. "We have to go," he said.

"Do you want your eggs scrambled or boiled?"

"Jack..."

"Alex. It's a ticket-only event. What will we do?"

"I'll work something out."

Jack scowled. "Are you really sure about this?"

"I know, Jack. It's Damian Cray. Everyone loves him. But here's something they may not have noticed." He folded the paper and slid it back to her. "The terrorist group that claimed responsibility for the bomb in France was called Camargue Sans Touristes."

"I know."

"And this new computer game has been developed by Cray Software Technology."

"What about it, Alex?"

"Maybe it's just another coincidence. But CST... It's the same letters."

Jack nodded. "All right," she said. "So how do we get in?"

They took a bus up to Knightsbridge and crossed over into Hyde Park. Before he had even passed through the gates and into the park itself, Alex could see just how much had been invested in the launch. There were hundreds of people streaming along the pavements, getting out of taxies and limousines, milling around in a crowd that seemed to cover every centimetre of grass. Policemen on foot and on horseback stood at every corner, giving directions and trying to form people into orderly lines. Alex was amazed that the horses could remain so calm surrounded by so much chaos.

And then there was the Pleasure Dome itself. It was as if a fantastic spaceship had landed in the middle of the lake at the centre of Hyde Park. It seemed to float on the surface of the water, a black pod, surrounded by a gleaming aluminium frame, silver rods criss-crossing in a dazzling pattern. Blue and red spotlights swivelled and rocked, the beams flashing even in the daylight. A single metal bridge stretched across from the bank to the entrance but there were more than a dozen security men barring the way. Nobody was allowed to cross the water without showing their ticket. There was no other way in.

Music blared out of hidden speakers: Cray singing from his last album, *White Lines*. Alex walked down to the edge of the water. He could hear shouting and, even in the hazy afternoon sun, he was almost blinded by a hundred flash-bulbs all exploding at the same time. The mayor of London had just arrived and was waving at the press pack, at least a hundred strong, herded together into a pen next to the bridge. Alex looked around and realized that he knew quite a few of the faces converging on the Pleasure Dome. There were actors, television presenters, models, DJs, politicians ... all waving their invitations and queuing up to be let in. This was more than the first appearance of a new game system. It was the most exclusive party London had ever seen.

And somehow he had to get in.

He ignored a policeman who was trying to move him out of the way and continued towards the bridge, walking confidently, as if he had been invited. Jack was a few steps away from him and he nodded at her.

It had been Ian Rider, of course, who had taught him the basics of pickpocketing. At the time it had just been a game, shortly after Alex's tenth birthday, when the two of them were together in Prague. They were talking about *Oliver Twist* and his uncle was explaining the techniques of the Artful Dodger, even providing his nephew with a quick demonstration. It was only much later that Alex had discovered that all this had been yet another aspect of his training; that all along his uncle had secretly been turning him into something he had never wanted to be.

But it would be useful now.

Alex was close to the bridge. He could see the invitations being checked by the burly men in their security uniforms: silver cards with the Gameslayer logo stamped in black. There was a natural crush here as the crowd arrived at the bottleneck and sorted itself into a single line to cross the bridge. He glanced one last time at Jack. She was ready.

Alex stopped.

"Somebody's stolen my ticket!" he shouted.

Even with the music pounding out, his voice was loud enough to carry to the crowd in the immediate area. It was a classic pickpocket's trick. Nobody cared about him, but suddenly they were worried about their own tickets. Alex saw one man pull open his jacket and glance into his inside pocket. Next to him a woman briefly opened and closed her handbag. Several people took their tickets out and clutched them tightly in their hands. A plump, bearded man reached round and tapped his back jeans pocket. Alex smiled. Now he knew where the tickets were.

He signalled to Jack. The plump man with the beard was going to be the mark – the one he had chosen. He was perfectly placed, just a few steps in front of Alex. And the corner of his ticket was actually visible, just poking out of the back pocket. Jack was going to play the part of the stall; Alex was in position to make the dip. Everything was set.

Jack walked ahead and seemed to recognize the man with the beard. "Harry!" she exclaimed, and threw her arms around him.

"I'm not..." the man began.

At that exact moment, Alex took two steps forward, swerved round a woman he vaguely recognized from a television drama series and slipped the ticket out of the man's pocket and placed it quickly under his own jacket, holding it in place with the side of his arm. It had taken less than three seconds and Alex hadn't even been particularly careful. This was the simple truth about pickpocketing. It demanded organization as much as skill. The mark was distracted. All his attention was on Jack, who was still embracing him. Pinch someone on the arm and they won't notice if, at the same time, you're touching their leg. That was what Ian Rider had taught Alex all those years ago.

"Don't you remember me?" Jack was exclaiming. "We met at the Savoy!"

"No. I'm sorry. You've got the wrong person."

Alex was already brushing past, on his way to the bridge. In a few moments the mark would reach for his ticket and find it missing, but even if he grabbed hold of Jack and accused her, there would be no evidence. Alex and the ticket would have disappeared.

He showed the ticket to a security man and stepped onto the bridge. Part of him felt bad about what he had done and he hoped the man with the beard would still be able to talk his way in. Quietly he cursed Damian Cray for turning him into a thief. But he knew that, from the moment Cray had answered his call in the South of France, there could be no going back.

He crossed the bridge and gave the ticket up on the other side. Ahead of him was a triangular entrance. Alex stepped forward and went into the dome: a huge area fitted out with high-tech lighting and a raised stage with a giant plasma screen displaying the letters CST. There were already about five hundred guests spread out in front of it, drinking champagne and eating canapés. Waiters were circulating with bottles and trays. A sense of excitement buzzed all around.

The music stopped. The lighting changed and the screen went blank. Then there was a low hum and clouds of dry ice began to pour onto the stage. A single word – GAMESLAYER – appeared on the screen; the hum grew louder. The Gameslayer letters broke up as an animated figure appeared, a ninja warrior, dressed in black from head to toe, clinging to the screen like a cutdown version of Spiderman. The hum was deafening now, a roaring desert wind with an orchestra somewhere behind. Hidden fans must have been turned on because real wind suddenly blasted through the dome, clearing away the smoke and revealing Damian Cray – in a white suit with a wide, pink and silver striped tie – standing alone on the stage, with his image, hugely magnified, on the screen behind.

The audience surged towards him, applauding. Cray raised a hand for silence.

"Welcome, welcome!" he said.

Alex found himself drawn towards the stage like everyone else. He wanted to get as close to Cray as he could. Already he was feeling that strange sensation of actually being in the same room as a man he had known all his life ... but a man he had never met. Damian Cray was smaller in real life than he seemed in his photographs. That was Alex's first thought. Nevertheless, Cray had been an A-list celebrity for thirty years. His presence was huge and he radiated confidence and control.

"Today is the day that I launch the Gameslayer, my new games console," Cray went on. He had a faint trace of an American accent. "I'd like to thank you all for coming. But if there's anyone here from Sony or Nintendo, I'm afraid I have bad news for you." He paused and smiled. "You're history."

There was laughter and applause from the audience. Even Alex found himself smiling. Cray had a way of including people, as if he personally knew everyone in the crowd.

"Gameslayer offers graphic quality and detail like no other system on the planet," Cray went on. "It can generate worlds, characters and totally complex physical simulations in real time thanks to the floating-point processing power of the system, which is, in a word, massive. Other systems give you plastic dolls fighting cardboard cut-outs. With Gameslayer, hair, eyes, skin tones, water, wood, metal and smoke all look like the real thing. We obey the rules of gravity and friction. More than that, we've built something into the system that we call pain synthesis. What does this mean? In a minute you'll find out."

He paused and the audience clapped again.

"Before I move on to the demonstration, I wonder if any of the journalists among you have any questions?"

A man near the front raised his hand. "How many games are you releasing this year?"

"Right now we only have the one game," Cray replied. "But there will be twelve more in the shops by Christmas."

"What is the first game called?" someone asked.

"Feathered Serpent."

"Is it a shoot-'em-up?" a woman asked.

"Well, yes. It is a stealth game," Cray admitted.

"So it involves shooting?"

"Yes."

The woman smiled, but not humorously. She was in her forties, with grey hair and a severe, schoolteacher face. "It's well known that you have a dislike of violence," she said. "So how can you justify selling children violent games?"

A ripple of unease ran through the audience. The woman might be a journalist, but somehow it seemed wrong to question Cray in this manner. Not when you were drinking his champagne and eating his food.

Cray, however, didn't seem offended. "That's a good question," he replied in his soft, lilting voice. "And I'll tell you, when we began with the Gameslayer, we did develop a game where the hero had to collect different-coloured flowers from a garden and then arrange them in vases. It had bunnies and egg sandwiches too. But do you know what? Our research team discovered that modern teenagers didn't want to play it. Can you imagine? They told me we wouldn't sell a single copy!"

Everyone broke into laughter. Now it was the female journalist who was looking uncomfortable.

Cray held up a hand again. "Actually, you've made a fair point," he went on. "It's true – I hate violence. Real violence ... war. But, you know, modern kids do have a lot of aggression in them. That's the truth of it. I suppose it's human nature. And I've come to think that it's better for them to get rid of that aggression playing harmless computer games, like mine, than out on the street."

"Your games still encourage violence!" the woman insisted.

Damian Cray frowned. "I think I've answered your question. So maybe you should stop questioning my answer," he said.

This was greeted by more applause, and Cray waited until it had died down. "But now, enough talk," he said. "I want you to see Gameslayer for yourself, and the best way to see it is to play it. I wonder if we have any teenagers in the audience, although now I come to think of it, I don't remember inviting any..."

"There's one here!" someone shouted, and Alex felt himself pushed forward. Suddenly everyone was looking at him and Cray himself was peering down from the stage.

"No..." Alex started to protest.

But the audience was already clapping, urging him on. A corridor opened up in front of him. Alex stumbled forward and before he knew it he was climbing up onto the stage. The room seemed to tilt. A spotlight spun round, dazzling him. And there it was.

He was standing on the stage with Damian Cray.

FEATHERED SERPENT

It was the last thing Alex could have expected.

He was face to face with the man who – if he was right – had ordered the death of Sabina's father. But *was* he right? For the first time, he was able to examine Cray at close quarters. It was a strangely unsettling experience.

Cray had one of the most famous faces in the world. Alex had seen it on CD covers, on posters, in newspapers and magazines, on television ... even on the back of cereal packets. And yet the face in front of him now was somehow disappointing. It was less real than all the images he had seen.

Cray was surprisingly young-looking, considering he was already in his fifties, but there was a taut, shiny quality to his skin that whispered of plastic surgery. And surely the neat, jet-black hair had to be dyed. Even the bright green eyes seemed somehow lifeless. Cray was a very small man. Alex found himself thinking of a doll in a toyshop. That was what Cray reminded him of. His superstardom and his millions of pounds had turned him into a plastic replica of himself.

And yet...

Cray had welcomed him onto the stage and was beaming at him as if he were an old friend. He was a singer. And, as he had made clear, he opposed violence. He wanted to save the world, not destroy it. MI6 had gathered files on him and found nothing. Alex was here because of a voice, a few words spoken at the end of a phone. He was beginning to wish he had never come.

It seemed that the two of them had been standing there for ages, up on the stage with hundreds of people waiting to see the demonstration. In fact, only a few seconds had passed. Then Cray held out a hand. "What's your name?" he asked.

"Alex Rider."

"Well, it's great to meet you, Alex Rider. I'm Damian Cray."

They shook hands. Alex couldn't help thinking that there were millions of people all around the world who would give anything to be where he was now.

"How old are you, Alex?" Cray asked.

"Fourteen."

"I'm very grateful to you for coming. Thanks for agreeing to help."

The words were being amplified around the dome. Out of the corner of his eye, Alex saw that his own image had joined Cray's on the giant screen. "We're very lucky that we do indeed have a teenager," Cray went on, addressing the audience. "So let's see how ... Alex ... gets on with the first level of Gameslayer One: Feathered Serpent."

As Cray spoke, three technicians came onto the stage, bringing with them a television monitor, a games console, a table and a chair. Alex realized that he was going to be asked to play the game in front of the audience – with his progress beamed up onto the plasma screen.

"Feathered Serpent is based on the Aztec civilization," Cray explained to the audience. "The Aztecs arrived in Mexico in 1195, but some claim that they had in fact come from another planet. It is on that planet that Alex is about to find himself. His mission is to find the four missing suns. But first he must enter the temple of Tlaloc, fight his way through five chambers and then throw himself into the pool of sacred flame. This will take him to the next level."

A fourth technician had come onto the stage, carrying a webcam. He stopped in front of Alex and quickly scanned him, pressed a button on the side of the camera and left. Cray waited until he had gone.

"You may have been wondering about the little black-suited figure that you saw on the screen," he said, once again taking the audience into his confidence. "His name is Omni, and he will be the hero of all the Gameslayer games. You may think him a little dull and unimaginative. But Omni is every boy and every girl in Britain. He is every child in the world ... and now I will show you why!"

The screen went blank, then burst into a digital whirl of colour. There was a deafening fanfare – not trumpets but some electronic equivalent – and the gates of a temple with a huge Aztec face cut into the wood appeared. Alex could tell at once that the graphic detail of the Gameslayer was better than anything he had ever seen, but a moment later the audience gasped with surprise and Alex perfectly understood why. A boy had walked onto the screen and was standing in front of the gates, awaiting his command. The boy was Omni. But he had changed. He was now wearing exactly the same clothes as Alex. He looked like Alex. More than that, he was Alex right down to the brown eyes and the hanging strands of fair hair.

Applause exploded around the room. Alex could see journalists scribbling in their notebooks or talking quickly into mobile phones, hoping to be the first with this incredible scoop. The food and the champagne had been forgotten. Cray's technology had created an avatar, an electronic double of him, making it possible for any player not just to play the game but to become part of it. Alex knew then that the Gameslayer would sell all over the world. Cray would make millions.

And twenty per cent of that would go to charity, he reminded himself.

Could this man really be his enemy?

Cray waited until everyone was quiet, and then he turned to Alex. "It's time to play," he said.

Alex sat down in front of the computer screen that the technicians had set up. He took hold of the controller and pressed with his left thumb. In front of him and on the giant plasma screen, his other self walked to the right. He stopped and turned himself the other way. The controller was incredibly sensitive. Alex almost felt like an Aztec god, in total control of his mortal self.

"Don't worry if you get killed on your first go," Cray said. "The console is faster than anything on the market and it may take you a while to get used to it. But we're all on your side, Alex. So – let's play Feathered Serpent! Let's see how far you can go!"

The temple gates opened.

Alex pressed down and on the screen his avatar walked forward and into a game environment that was alien and bizarre and brilliantly realized. The temple was a fusion of primitive art and science fiction, with towering columns, flaming beacons, complex hieroglyphics and crouching Aztec statues. But the floor was silver, not stone. Strange metal stairways and corridors twisted around the temple area. Electric light flickered behind heavily barred windows. Closed-circuit cameras followed his every move.

"You have to start by finding two weapons in the first chamber," Cray advised, leaning over Alex's shoulder. "You may need them later."

The first chamber was huge, with organ music throbbing and stained-glass windows showing cornfields, crop circles and hovering spaceships. Alex found the first weapon easily enough. There was a sword hanging high up on a wall. But he soon realized there were traps everywhere. Part of the wall crumbled as he climbed it and reaching out for the sword activated a missile which shot out of nowhere, aiming for the avatar. The missile was a double boomerang with razor-blade edges, rotating at lightning speed. Alex knew that if he was hit, he would be cut in half.

He stabbed down with his thumbs and his miniature self crouched. The boomerang spun past. But as it went, one of its blades caught the avatar on the arm. The audience gasped. A tiny flow of blood had appeared on the miniature figure's sleeve and its face – *Alex's* face – had distorted, showing pain. The experience was so realistic that Alex almost felt a need to check his own, real arm. He had to remind himself that it was only the avatar that had been wounded.

"Pain synthesis!" Cray repeated the words, his voice echoing across the Pleasure Dome. "In the Gameslayer world, we share all the hero's emotions. And should Alex die, the central processing unit will ensure that we feel his death."

Alex had climbed back down and was searching for the second weapon. The little wound was already healing, the blood flow slowing down. He dodged as another boomerang shot past his shoulder. But he still couldn't find the second weapon.

"Try looking behind the ivy," Cray suggested in a stage whisper, and the audience smiled, amused that Alex needed help so soon.

There was a crossbow concealed in an alcove. But what Cray hadn't told Alex was that the ivy covering the alcove contained a ten thousand volt charge. He found out soon enough. The moment his avatar touched the ivy, there was a blue flash and it was thrown backwards, screaming out loud, its eyes wide and staring. The avatar hadn't quite been killed, but it had been badly hurt.

Cray tapped Alex on the shoulder. "You'll have to be more careful than that," he said.

A buzz of excitement travelled through the audience. They had never seen anything like this before.

And that was when Alex decided. Suddenly MI6, Yassen, Saint-Pierre ... all of it was forgotten. Cray had tricked him into touching the ivy. He had deliberately injured him. Of course, it was just a game. It was only the avatar that had been hurt. But the humiliation had been his – and suddenly he was determined to get the better of Feathered Serpent. He wasn't going to be beaten. He wasn't going to share his death with anyone.

Grimly, he picked up the crossbow and sent the avatar forward, further into the Aztec world.

The second chamber consisted of a huge hole in the ground. It was actually a pit, fifty metres deep, with narrow pillars stretching all the way to the top. The only way to get from one side to the other was to jump from one pillar to the next. If he missed his step or overbalanced, he would fall to his death – and to make it more difficult it was pouring with rain inside the chamber, making the surfaces slippery. The rain itself was extraordinary. As Cray told the audience, the Gameslayer's image technology allowed every raindrop to be realized individually. The avatar was soaking wet, its clothes sodden and its hair plastered to its head.

There was a sudden electronic squawk. A creature with butterfly wings and the face and claws of a dragon swooped down, trying to knock the avatar off its perch. Alex brought the crossbow up and shot it, then took the last three leaps to the other side of the pit.

"You're doing very well," Damian Cray said. "But I wonder if you'll make it through the third chamber."

Alex was confident. Feathered Serpent was beautifully designed. Its texture maps and backgrounds were perfect. The Omni character was way ahead of the competition. But for all this, it was just another computer game, similar to ones that Alex had played on Xbox and PlayStation 2. He knew what he was doing. He could win.

He made easy work of the third section: a tall, narrow corridor with carved faces on either side. A hail of wooden spears and arrows fired out of the wooden mouths but not one of them came close as the avatar ducked and weaved, all the time running forward. A bubbling river of acid twisted along the corridor. The avatar jumped over it as if it were a harmless stream.

Now he came to an incredible indoor jungle where the greatest threat, among the trees and the creepers, was a huge robotic snake, covered in spikes. The creature looked horrific. Alex had never seen better graphics. But his avatar ran circles round it, leaving it behind so quickly that the audience barely had a chance to see it.

Cray's face hadn't changed, but now he was leaning over Alex, his eyes fixed on the screen, one hand resting on Alex's shoulder. His knuckles were almost white.

"You're making it look too easy," he murmured.

Although the words were spoken light-heartedly, there was a rising tension in his voice.

Because the audience was now on Alex's side. Millions of pounds had been spent on the development of the Feathered Serpent software. But it was being beaten by the first teenager to play it. As Alex dodged a second robotic snake, someone laughed. The hand on his shoulder tightened.

He came to the fifth chamber. This was a mirror maze, filled with smoke and guarded by a dozen Aztec gods wrapped in feathers, jewellery and golden masks. Again, each and every one of the gods was a small masterpiece of graphic art. But although they lunged at the avatar, they kept on missing, and suddenly more of the people in the audience were laughing and applauding, urging Alex on.

One more god, this one with claws and an alligator tail, stood between Alex and the pool of fire that would lead him to the next level. All he had to do was get past it. That was when Cray made his move. He was careful. Nobody would see what happened and if they did it would simply look as if he was carried away by the excitement of the game. But he was quite deliberate. His hand suddenly moved to Alex's arm and closed tight, pulling it away from the controller. For a few brief seconds, Alex lost control. It was enough. The Aztec god reached out and its claws raked across the avatar's stomach. Alex actually heard his shirt being torn; he almost felt the pain as the blood poured out. His avatar fell to its knees, then pitched forward and lay still. The screen froze and the words **GAME OVER** appeared in red letters.

Silence fell inside the dome.

"Too bad, Alex," Cray said. "I'm afraid it wasn't quite as easy as you thought."

There was a scattering of applause from the audience. It was hard to tell if they were applauding the technology of the game or the way Alex had taken it on and almost beaten it. But there was also a sense of unease. Perhaps Feathered Serpent was too realistic. It really was as if a part of Alex had died there, on the screen.

Alex turned to Cray. He was angry. He alone knew that the man had cheated. But Cray was smiling again.

"You did great," he said. "I asked for a demonstration and you certainly gave us one. You make sure you leave your address with one of my assistants. I'll be sending you a free Gameslayer system and all the introductory games."

The audience heard this and applauded with more enthusiasm. For a second time, Cray held out a hand. Alex hesitated for a moment, then took it. In a way, he couldn't blame Cray. The man couldn't allow the Gameslayer to be turned into a laughing stock on its first outing. He had an investment to protect. But Alex still didn't like what had happened.

"Good to meet you, Alex. Well done..."

He climbed down from the stage. There were more demonstrations and more talks by members of Cray's staff. Then lunch was served. But Alex didn't eat. He had seen enough. He left the Pleasure Dome and crossed over the water, walking back through the park and all the way down to the King's Road.

Jack was waiting for him when he got home.

"So how did it go?" she asked.

Alex told her.

"What a cheater!" Jack scowled. "Mind you, Alex. A lot of rich men are bad losers and Cray is very rich indeed. Do you really think this proves anything?"

"I don't know, Jack." Alex was confused. He had to remind himself: a great chunk of the Gameslayer profits was going to charity. A huge amount. And he still had no proof. A few words on a phone. Was it enough to tie Cray in with what had happened in Saint-Pierre? "Maybe we should go to Paris," he said. "That was where this all began. There was a meeting. Edward Pleasure was there. He was working with a photographer. Sabina told me his name. Marc Antonio."

"With a name like that, he should be easy enough to track down," Jack said. "And I love Paris."

"It still might be a waste of time." Alex sighed. "I didn't like Damian Cray. But now that I've met him..." His voice trailed off. "He's an entertainer. He makes computer games. He didn't look like the sort of man who'd want to hurt anyone."

"It's your call, Alex."

Alex shook his head. "I don't know, Jack. I just don't know..."

The launch of the Gameslayer was on the news that night. According to the reports, the entire industry had been knocked out by the graphic quality and the processing power of the new system. The part that Alex had played in the demonstration wasn't mentioned. However, something else was.

An event had taken place that had cast a cloud over what would otherwise have been a perfect day. It seemed that someone had died. A picture flashed up onto the screen, a woman's face, and

Alex recognized her at once. It was the school-teacherly woman who had put Cray on the spot, asking him awkward questions about violence. A policeman explained that she had been run over by a car as she left Hyde Park. The driver hadn't stopped.

The following morning Alex and Jack went to Waterloo and bought two tickets for Eurostar.

By lunchtime they were in Paris.

RUE BRITANNIA

"Do you realize, Alex," Jack said, "Picasso sat exactly where we're sitting now. And Chagall. And Salvador Dalí..."

"At this very table?"

"At this very café. All the big artists came here."

"What are you trying to say, Jack?"

"Well, I was just wondering if you'd like to forget this whole adventure thing and come with me to the Picasso Museum. Paris is such a fun place. And I've always found looking at pictures a lot more enjoyable than getting shot."

"Nobody's shooting at us."

"Yet."

A day had passed since they had arrived in Paris and booked into a little hotel that Jack knew, opposite Notre-Dame. Jack knew the city well. She had once spent a year at the Sorbonne, studying art. But for the death of Ian Rider and her involvement with Alex, she might well have gone to live there.

She had been right about one thing. Finding out where Marc Antonio lived had been easy enough. She had only telephoned three agencies before she found the one that represented the photographer, although it had taken all her charm – and rusty French – to cajole his telephone number out of the girl on the switchboard. Getting to meet him, however, was proving more difficult.

She had rung the number a dozen times during the course of the morning before it was answered. It was a man's voice. No, he wasn't Marc Antonio. Yes, this was Marc Antonio's house but he had no idea where he was. The voice was full of suspicion. Alex had been listening, sharing the receiver with Jack. In the end he took over.

"Listen," he said. His French was almost as good as Jack's, but then he had started learning when he was three years old. "My name is Alex Rider. I'm a friend of Edward Pleasure. He's an English journalist—"

"I know who he is."

"Do you know what happened to him?"

A pause. "Go on..."

"I have to speak to Marc Antonio. I have some important information." Alex considered for a moment. Should he tell this man what he knew? "It's about Damian Cray," he said.

The name seemed to have an effect. There was another pause, longer this time. Then...

"Come to la Palette. It's a café on the rue de Seine. I will meet you there at one o'clock."

There was a click as the man hung up.

It was now ten past one. La Palette was a small, bustling café on the corner of a square, surrounded by art galleries. Waiters with long white aprons were sweeping in and out, carrying trays laden with drinks high above their heads. The place was packed but Alex and Jack had managed to get a table right on the edge, where they would be most conspicuous. Jack was drinking a glass of beer; Alex had a bright red fruit juice – a *sirop de grenadine* – with ice. It was his favourite drink when he was in France.

He was beginning to wonder if the man he had spoken to on the telephone was going to show up. Or could he be here already? How were they going to find each other in this crowd? Then he noticed a motorcyclist sitting on a beaten-up

Piaggio 125cc motorbike on the other side of the street; he was a young man in a leather jacket with black curly hair and stubble on his cheeks. He had pulled in a few minutes before but hadn't dismounted, as if he was waiting for someone. Alex met his eye; there was a flash of contact. The young man looked puzzled but then he got off his bike and came over, moving warily as if afraid of a trap.

"You are Alex Rider?" he asked. He spoke English with an attractive accent, like an actor in a film.

"Yes."

"I wasn't expecting a child."

"What difference does it make?" Jack demanded, coming to Alex's defence. "Are you Marc Antonio?" she asked.

"No. My name is Robert Guppy."

"Do you know where he is?"

"He asked me to take you to him." Guppy glanced back at the Piaggio. "But I have only room for one."

"Well, you can forget it. I'm not letting Alex go on his own."

"It's all right, Jack," Alex cut in. He smiled at her. "It looks like you get to visit the Picasso Museum after all."

Jack sighed. Then she nodded. "All right," she said. "But take care."

Robert Guppy drove through Paris like someone who knew the city well – or who wanted to die in it. He swerved in and out of the traffic, ignored red lights and spun across intersections with the blare of car horns echoing all around. Alex found himself clinging on for dear life. He had no idea where they were going but realized there was a reason for Guppy's dangerous driving. He was making sure they weren't being followed.

They slowed down on the other side of the Seine, on the edge of the Marais, close to the Forum des Halles. Alex recognized the area. The last time he had been here, he had called himself Alex Friend and had been accompanying the hideous Mrs Stellenbosch on the way to the Point Blanc Academy. Now they slowed down and stopped in a street of typically Parisian houses – six storeys high with solid-looking doorways and tall frosted windows. Alex noticed a street sign: rue Britannia. The street went nowhere and half the buildings looked empty and dilapidated. Indeed, the ones at the far end were shored up by scaffolding and surrounded by wheelbarrows and cement mixers, with a plastic chute for debris.

But there were no workmen in sight.

Guppy got off the bike. He gestured at one of the doors. "This way," he said. He glanced up and down the street one last time, then led Alex in.

The door led to an inner courtyard with old furniture and a tangle of rusting bicycles in one corner. Alex followed Guppy up a short flight of steps and through another doorway. He found himself in a large, high-ceilinged room with whitewashed walls, windows on both sides and a dark wood floor. It was a photographer's studio. There were screens, complicated lamps on metal legs and silver umbrellas. But someone was also living here. To one side was a kitchen area with a pile of tins and dirty plates.

Robert Guppy closed the door and a man appeared from behind one of the screens. He was barefoot, wearing a string vest and shapeless jeans. Alex guessed he must be about fifty. He was thin, unshaven, with a tangle of hair that was black mixed with silver. Strangely, he only had one eye; the other was behind a patch. A one-eyed photographer? Alex couldn't see why not.

The man glanced at him curiously, then spoke to his friend.

"*C'est lui qui a téléphoné?*"

"*Oui...*"

"Are you Marc Antonio?" Alex asked.

"Yes. You say you are a friend of Edward Pleasure. I didn't know Edward hung out with kids."

"I know his daughter. I was staying with him in France when..." Alex hesitated. "You know what happened to him?"

"Of course I know what happened to him. Why do you think I am hiding here?" He gazed at Alex quizzically, his one good eye slowly evaluating him. "You said on the telephone that you could tell me something about Damian Cray. Do you know him?"

"I met him two days ago. In London..."

"Cray is no longer in London." It was Robert Guppy who spoke, leaning against the door. "He has a software plant just outside Amsterdam. In Sloterdijk. He arrived there this morning."

"How do you know?"

"We're keeping a close eye on Mr Cray."

Alex turned to Marc Antonio. "You have to tell me what you and Edward Pleasure found out about him," he said. "What story were you working on? What was the secret meeting he had here?"

The photographer thought for a moment, then

smiled crookedly, showing nicotine-stained teeth. "Alex Rider," he muttered, "you're a strange kid. You say you have information to give me, but you come here and you ask only questions. You have a nerve. But I like that." He took out a cigarette – a Gauloise – and screwed it into his mouth. He lit it and blew blue smoke into the air. "All right. It is against my better judgement. But I will tell you what I know."

There were two bar stools next to the kitchen. He perched on one and invited Alex to do the same. Robert Guppy stayed by the door.

"The story that Ed was working on had nothing to do with Damian Cray," he began. "At least, not to start with. Ed was never interested in the entertainment business. No. He was working on something much more important ... a story about the NSA. You know what that is? It's the National Security Agency of America. It's an organization involved in counter-terrorism, espionage and the protection of information. Most of its work is top secret. Code makers. Code breakers. Spies...

"Ed became interested in a man called Charlie Roper, an extremely high-ranking officer in the NSA. He had information – I don't know how he got it – that this man, Roper, might have turned traitor. He was heavily in debt. An addict..."

"Drugs?" Alex asked.

Marc Antonio shook his head. "Gambling. It can be just as destructive. Ed heard that Roper was here in Paris and believed he had come to sell secrets – either to the Chinese or, more likely, the North Koreans. He met me just over a week ago. We'd worked together often, he and I. He got the stories; I got the pictures. We were a team. More than that – we were friends." Marc Antonio shrugged. "Anyway, we found out where Roper was staying and we followed him from his hotel. We had no idea who he was meeting, and if you had told me, I would never have believed it."

He paused and drew on his Gauloise. The tip glowed red. Smoke trickled up in front of his good eye.

"Roper went for lunch at a restaurant called la Tour d'Argent. It is one of the most expensive restaurants in Paris. And it was Damian Cray who was paying the bill. We saw the two of them together. The restaurant is high up but it has wide glass windows with views of Paris. I took photographs of them with a telescopic lens. Cray gave Roper an envelope. I think it contained money, and, if so, it was a lot of money because the envelope was very thick."

"Wait a minute," Alex interrupted. "What would a pop singer want with someone from the NSA?"

"That is exactly what Ed wanted to know," the photographer replied. "He began to ask questions. He must have asked too many. Because the next thing I heard, someone had tried to kill him in Saint-Pierre and that same day they came for me. In my case the bomb was in my car. If I had turned the ignition, I wouldn't be speaking to you now."

"Why didn't you?"

"I am a careful man. I noticed a wire." He stubbed out the cigarette. "Someone also broke into my apartment. Much of my equipment was stolen, including my camera and all the photographs I had taken at la Tour d'Argent. It was no coincidence."

He paused.

"But why am I telling you all this, Alex Rider? Now it is your turn to tell me what you know."

"I was on holiday in Saint-Pierre—" Alex began.

That was as far as he got.

A car had stopped somewhere outside the building. Alex hadn't heard it approach. He only became aware of it when its engine stopped. Robert Guppy took a step forward, raising a hand.

Marc Antonio's head snapped round. There was a moment's silence – and Alex knew that it was the wrong sort of silence. It was empty. Final.

And then there was an explosion of bullets and the windows shattered, one after another, the glass falling in great slabs to the floor. Robert Guppy was killed instantly, thrown off his feet with a series of red holes stitched across his chest. A light bulb was hit and exploded; chunks of plaster crumbled off the wall. The air rushed in, and with it came the sound of men shouting and footsteps stamping across the courtyard.

Marc Antonio was the first to recover. Sitting by the kitchen, he had been out of the line of fire and hadn't been hit. Alex too was shocked but uninjured.

"This way!" the photographer shouted and propelled Alex across the room even as the door burst open with a crash of splintering wood. Alex just had time to glimpse a man dressed in black with a machine gun cradled in his arms. Then he was pulled behind one of the screens he had noticed earlier. There was another exit here – not a door but a jagged hole in the wall. Marc Antonio had already climbed through. Alex followed.

"Up!" Marc Antonio pushed Alex ahead of him. "It's the only way!"

There was a wooden staircase, seemingly unused, old and covered in plaster dust. Alex started to climb ... three floors, four, with Marc Antonio just behind him. There was a single door on each floor but Marc Antonio urged him on. He could hear the man with the machine gun. He had been joined by someone else. The two killers were following them up.

He arrived at the top. Another door barred his way. He reached out and turned the handle and at that moment there was another burst of gunfire and Marc Antonio grunted and curved away, falling backwards. Alex knew he was dead. Mercifully, the door had opened in front of him. He tumbled through, expecting at any moment to feel the rake of bullets across his shoulders. But the photographer had saved him, falling between Alex and his pursuers. Alex had made it onto the roof of the building. He lashed out with his heel, slamming the door shut behind him.

He found himself in a landscape of skylights and chimney stacks, water tanks and TV aerials. The roofs ran the full length of the rue Britannia, with low walls and thick pipes dividing the different houses. What had Marc Antonio intended, coming up here? He was six floors above street level. Was there a fire escape? A staircase leading down?

Alex had no time to find out. The door flew open and the two men came through it, moving more slowly now, knowing he was trapped. Somewhere deep inside Alex a voice whispered – why couldn't they leave him alone? They had come for Marc Antonio, not for him. He was nothing to do with this. But he knew they would have their orders. Kill the photographer and anyone associated with him. It didn't matter who Alex was. He was just part of the package.

And then he remembered something he had seen when he entered the rue Britannia, and suddenly he was running, without even being sure that he was going in the right direction. He heard the clatter of machine-gun fire and black tiles disintegrated centimetres behind his feet. Another burst. He felt a spray of bullets passing close to him and part of a chimney stack shattered, showering him with dust. He jumped over a low partition. The edge of the roof was getting closer. The men behind him paused, thinking he had nowhere to go. Alex kept running. He reached the edge and launched himself into the air.

To the men with the guns it must have seemed that he had jumped to a certain death on the pavement six floors below. But Alex had seen building works: scaffolding, cement mixers – and an orange pipe designed to carry builders' debris from the different floors down to the street.

The pipe actually consisted of a series of buckets, each one bottomless, interlocking like a flume at a swimming pool. Alex couldn't judge his leap – but he was lucky. For a second or two he fell, arms and legs sprawling. Then he saw the entrance to the pipe and managed to steer himself towards it. First his outstretched legs, then his hips and shoulders, entered the tube perfectly. The tunnel was filled with cement dust and he was blinded. He could just make out the orange walls flashing past. The back of his head, his thighs and shoulders were battered mercilessly. He couldn't breathe and realized with a sick dread that if the exit was blocked he would break every bone in his body.

The tube was shaped like a stretched-out J. As Alex reached the bottom, he felt himself slowing down. Suddenly he was spat back out into daylight. There was a mound of sand next to one of the cement mixers and he thudded into it. All the breath was knocked out of him. Sand and cement filled his mouth. But he was alive.

Painfully he got to his feet and looked up. The two men were still on the roof, far above him.

They had decided not to attempt his stunt. The orange tube had been just wide enough to take him; they would have got jammed before they were halfway. Alex looked up the street. There was a car parked outside the entrance to Marc Antonio's studio. But there was nobody in sight.

He spat and dragged the back of his hand across his lips; then he limped quickly away. Marc Antonio was dead, but he had given Alex another piece of the puzzle. And Alex knew where he had to go next. Sloterdijk. A software plant outside Amsterdam. Just a few hours on a train from Paris.

He reached the end of the rue Britannia and turned the corner, moving faster all the time. He was bruised, filthy and lucky to be alive. He just wondered how he was going to explain all this to Jack.

BLOOD MONEY

Alex lay on his stomach, watching the guards as they examined the waiting car. He was holding a pair of Bausch & Lomb prism system binoculars with 30x magnification, and although he was more than a hundred metres away from the main gate, he could see everything clearly ... right down to the car's number plate and the driver's moustache.

He had been here for more than an hour, lying motionless in front of a bank of pine trees, hidden from sight by a row of shrubs. He was wearing grey jeans, a dark T-shirt and a khaki jacket, which he had picked up in the same army supplies shop that had provided the binoculars. The weather had turned yet again, bringing with it an afternoon of constant drizzle, and Alex was soaked through. He wished now that he had brought the thermos of hot chocolate Jack had offered him. At the time, he'd thought she was treating him like a child – but even the SAS know the importance of keeping warm. They had taught him as much when he was training with them.

Jack had come with him to Amsterdam and once again it had been she who had checked them into a hotel, this time on the Herengracht, one of the three main canals. She was there now, waiting in their room. Of course, she had wanted to come with him. After what had happened in Paris, she was more worried about him than ever. But Alex had persuaded her that two people would have twice as much chance of being spotted as one, and her bright red hair would hardly help. Reluctantly she had agreed.

"Just make sure you get back to the hotel before dark," she said. "And if you pass a tulip shop, maybe you could bring me a bunch."

He smiled, remembering her words. He shifted his weight, feeling the damp grass beneath his elbows. He wondered what exactly he had learnt in the past hour.

He was in the middle of a strange industrial area on the outskirts of Amsterdam. Sloterdijk contained a sprawl of factories, warehouses and processing plants. Most of the compounds were low-rise, separated from each other by wide stretches of tarmac, but there were also clumps of trees and grassland as if someone had tried – and failed – to cheer the place up. Three windmills rose up behind the headquarters of Cray's technological empire. But they weren't the traditional Dutch models, the sort that would appear on picture postcards. These were modern, towering pillars of grey concrete with triple blades endlessly slicing the air. They were huge and menacing, like invaders from another planet.

The compound itself reminded Alex of an army barracks ... or maybe a prison. It was surrounded by a double fence, the outer one topped with razor wire. There were guard towers at fifty-metre intervals and guards on patrol all around the perimeter. In Holland, a country where the police carry guns, Alex wasn't surprised that the guards were armed. Inside, he could make out eight or nine buildings, low and rectangular, white-bricked with high-tech plastic roofs. Various people were moving around, some of them transported in electric cars. Alex could hear the whine of the engines, like milk floats. The compound had its own communications centre, with five huge satellite dishes mounted outside. Otherwise, it seemed to consist of laboratories, offices and living quarters. One building stood out in the middle of it all: a glass and steel cube, aggressively modern in design. This might be the main headquarters, Alex thought. Perhaps he would find Damian Cray inside.

But how was he to get in? He had been studying the entrance for the last hour.

A single road led up to the gate, with a traffic light at each end. It was a complicated process. When a car or a truck arrived, it stopped at the bottom of the road and waited. Only when the first traffic light changed was it allowed to continue forward to the glass and brick guardhouse next to the gate. At this point, a uniformed man appeared and took the driver's ID, presumably to check it on a computer. Two more men examined the vehicle, checking that there were no passengers. And that wasn't all. There was a security camera mounted high up on the fence and Alex had noticed a length of what looked like toughened glass built into the road. When the vehicles stopped they were right on top of it, and Alex guessed that there must be a second camera underneath. There was no way he could sneak into the compound. Cray Software Technology had left nothing to chance.

Several trucks had entered the compound while he had been watching. Alex had recognized the black-clothed figure of Omni painted – life-sized – on the sides as part of the Gameslayer logo. He wondered if it might be possible to sneak inside one of the trucks, perhaps as it was waiting at the first set of lights. But the road was too open. At night it would be floodlit. Anyway, the doors would almost certainly be locked.

He couldn't climb the fences. The razor wire would see to that. He doubted he could tunnel his way in. Could he somehow disguise himself and mingle with the evening shift? No. For once his size and age were against him. Maybe Jack would have been able to attempt it, pretending to be a replacement cleaner or a technician. But there was no way he would be able to talk his way past the guards, particularly without speaking a word of Dutch. Security was too tight.

And then Alex saw it. Right in front of his eyes.

Another truck had stopped and the driver was being questioned while the cabin was searched. Could he do it? He remembered the bicycle that was chained to a lamppost just a couple of hundred metres down the road. Before he had left England he had gone through the manual that had come with it and had been amazed how many gadgets Smithers had been able to conceal in and around such an ordinary object. Even the bicycle clips were magnetic! Alex watched the gate slide open and the truck pass through.

Yes. It would work. He would have to wait until it was dark – but it was the last thing anyone would expect. Despite everything, Alex suddenly found himself smiling.

He just hoped he could find a fancy-dress shop in Amsterdam.

By nine o'clock it was dark but the searchlights around the compound had been activated long before, turning the area into a dazzling collision of black and white. The gates, the razor wire, the guards with their guns … all could be seen a mile away. But now they were throwing vivid shadows, pools of darkness that might offer a hiding place to anyone brave enough to get close.

A single truck was approaching the main gate. The driver was Dutch and had driven up from the port of Rotterdam. He had no idea what he was carrying and he didn't care. From the first day he had started working for Cray Software Technology, he had known that it was better not to ask questions. The first of the two traffic lights was red and he slowed down, then came to a halt. There were no other vehicles in sight and he was annoyed to be kept waiting, but it was better not to complain. There was a sudden knocking sound and he glanced out of the window, looking in the side mirror. Was someone trying to get his attention? But there was no one there and a moment later the light changed, so he threw the gearstick into first and moved on again.

As usual he drove onto the glass panel and wound down his window. There was a guard standing outside and he passed across his ID, a plastic card with his photograph, name and employee number. The driver knew that other guards would inspect his truck. He sometimes wondered why they were so sensitive about security. After all, they were only making computer games. But he had heard about industrial sabotage ... companies stealing secrets from each other. He supposed it made sense.

Two guards were walking round the truck even as the driver sat there, thinking his private thoughts. A third was examining the pictures being transmitted by the camera underneath it. The truck had recently been cleaned. The word GAMESLAYER stood out on the side, with the Omni figure crouching next to it. One of the guards reached out and tried to open the door at the back. It was, as it should have been, locked. Meanwhile the other guard peered in through the front cabin window. But it was obvious that the driver was alone.

The security operation was smooth and well practised. The cameras had shown nobody hiding underneath the truck or on the roof. The rear door was locked. The driver had been cleared. One of the guards gave a signal and the gate opened electronically, sliding sideways to let the truck in. The driver knew where to go without being told. After about fifty metres he branched off the entrance road and followed a narrower track that brought him to the unloading bay. There were about a dozen other vehicles parked here, with warehouses on both sides. The driver turned off the engine, got out and locked the door. He had paperwork to deal with. He would hand over the keys and receive a stamped docket with his time of arrival. They would unload the vehicle the following day.

The driver left. Nothing moved. There was nobody else in the area.

But if anyone had walked past, they might have seen a remarkable thing. On the side of the truck, the black-clothed figure of Omni turned its head. At least, that was what it would have looked like. But if that person had looked more closely, they would have realized that there were two figures on the truck. One was painted; the other was a real person, clinging impossibly to the metal panelling in exactly the same position as the picture underneath.

Alex Rider dropped silently to the ground. The muscles in his arms and legs were screaming and he wondered how much longer he would have been able to hold on. Smithers had supplied four powerful magnetic clips with the bike and these were what Alex had used to keep himself in place: two for his hands, two for his feet. He quickly pulled off the black ninja suit he had bought that afternoon in Amsterdam, rolled it up and stuffed it into a bin. He had been in plain sight of the guards as the truck drove through the gate. But the guards hadn't looked too closely. They had expected to see a figure next to the Gameslayer logo and that was just what they had seen. For once they had been wrong to believe their eyes.

Alex took stock of his surroundings. He might be inside the compound, but his luck wouldn't last for ever. He didn't doubt that there would be other guards on patrol, and other cameras too. What exactly was he looking for? The strange thing was, he had no real idea. But something told him that if Damian Cray went in for all this security, then it must be because he had something to hide. Of course, it was still possible that Alex was wrong, that Cray was innocent. It was a comforting thought.

He made his way through the compound, heading for the great cube that stood at its heart. He heard a whining sound and ducked into the shadows next to a wall as an electronic car sped past with three passengers and a woman in blue overalls at the wheel. He became aware of activity somewhere ahead of him. An open area, brilliantly lit, stretched out behind one of the warehouses. A voice suddenly echoed in the air, amplified by a speaker system. It was a man speaking – but in Dutch. Alex couldn't understand a word. Moving more quickly, he hurried on, determined to see what was happening.

He found a narrow alleyway between two of the buildings and ran the full length, grateful for the shadows of the walls. At the end he came to a fire escape, a metal staircase spiralling upwards, and threw himself breathlessly behind it. He could hide here. But, looking between the steps, he had a clear view of what was happening ahead.

There was a square of black tarmac with glass and steel office blocks on all sides. The largest of these was the cube that Alex had seen from outside. Damian Cray was standing in front of it, talking animatedly to a man in a white coat, with three more men just behind him. Even from a distance Cray was unmistakable. He was the smallest person there, dressed in yet another designer suit. He had come out to watch some sort of demonstration. About half a dozen guards stood waiting, dotted around the square. Harsh white lights were being beamed down from two metal towers that Alex hadn't noticed before.

Watching through the fire escape, Alex saw that there was a cargo plane in the middle of the square. It took him a moment or two to accept what he was seeing. There was no way the plane could have landed there. The square was only just wide enough to contain it, and there wasn't a runway inside the compound, as far as he knew. It must have been carried here on a truck, possibly assembled on site. But what was it doing here? The plane was an old-fashioned one. It had propellers rather than jets, and wings high up, almost sitting on top of the main body. The words MILLENNIUM AIR were painted in red along the fuselage and on the tail.

Cray looked at his watch. A minute later the loudspeaker crackled again with another announcement in Dutch. Everyone stopped talking and gazed at the plane. Alex stared. A fire had started inside the main cabin. He could see the flames flickering behind the windows. Grey smoke began to seep out of the fuselage and suddenly one of the propellers caught alight. The fire seemed to spread out of control in seconds, consuming the engine and then spreading across the wing. Alex waited for someone to do something. If there was any fuel in the plane, it would surely explode at any moment. But nobody moved. Cray seemed to nod.

It was over as quickly as it had begun. The man in the white coat spoke into a radio transmitter and the fire went out. It was extinguished so quickly that if Alex hadn't seen it with his own eyes, he wouldn't have believed it had been there in the first place. They didn't use water or foam. There were no scorch marks and no smoke.

One moment the plane had been burning; the next it wasn't. It was as simple as that.

Cray and the three men with him spent a few seconds talking, before turning and strolling back into the cube. The guards in the square marched off. The plane was left where it was. Alex wondered what on earth he had got himself into. This had nothing to do with computer games. It made absolutely no sense at all.

But at least he had spotted Damian Cray.

Alex waited until the guards had gone, then twisted out from behind the fire escape. He made his way as quickly as he could around the square, keeping in the shadows. Cray had made a mistake. Breaking into the compound was virtually impossible, so he had worried less about security on the inside. Alex hadn't spotted any cameras, and the guards in the towers were looking out rather than in. For the moment he was safe.

He followed Cray into the building and found himself crossing the white marble floor of what was nothing more than a huge glass box. Above him he could see the night sky with the three windmills looming in the distance. The building contained nothing. But there was a single round hole in one corner of the floor and a staircase leading down.

Alex heard voices.

He crept down the stairs, which led directly into a large underground room. Crouching on the bottom step, concealed behind wide steel banisters, he watched.

The room was open-plan, with a white marble

floor and corridors leading off in several directions. The architecture made him think of a vault in an ultra-modern bank. But the gorgeous rugs, the fireplace, the Italian furniture and the dazzling white Bechstein grand piano could have come out of a palace. To one side was a curving desk with a bank of telephones and computer screens. All the lighting was at floor level, giving the room a bizarre, unsettling atmosphere, with all the shadows going the wrong way. A portrait of Damian Cray holding a white poodle covered an entire wall.

The man himself was sitting on a sofa, sipping a bright yellow drink. He had a cherry on a cocktail stick and Alex watched him pick it off with his perfect white teeth and slowly eat it. The three men from the square were with him, and Alex knew at once that he had been right all along – that Cray was indeed at the centre of the web.

One of the men was Yassen Gregorovich. Wearing jeans and a polo neck, he was sitting on the piano stool, his legs crossed. The second man stood near him, leaning against the piano. He was older, with silver hair and a sagging, pock-marked face. He was wearing a blue blazer with a striped tie that made him look like a minor official in a bank or a cricket club. He had large spectacles that had sunk into his face as if it were damp clay. He looked nervous, the eyes behind the glass circles blinking frequently. The third man was darkly handsome, in his late forties, with black hair, grey eyes and a jawline that was square and serious. He was casually dressed in a leather jacket and an open-necked shirt and seemed to be enjoying himself.

Cray was talking to him. "I'm very grateful to you, Mr Roper. Thanks to you, Eagle Strike can now proceed on schedule."

Roper! This was the man Cray had met in Paris. Alex had a sense that everything had come full circle. He strained to hear what the two men were saying.

"Hey – please. Call me Charlie." The man spoke with an American accent. "And there's no need to thank me, Damian. I've enjoyed doing business with you."

"I do have a few questions," Cray murmured, and Alex saw him pick up an object from a coffee table next to the sofa. It was a metallic capsule, about the same shape and size as a mobile phone. "As I understand it, the gold codes change daily. Presumably the flash drive is currently programmed with today's codes. But if Eagle

Strike were to take place two days from now..."

"Just plug it in. The flash drive will update itself," Roper explained. He had an easy, lazy smile. "That's the beauty of it. First it will burrow through the security systems. Then it will pick up the new codes ... like taking candy from a baby. The moment you have the codes, you transmit them back through Milstar and you're set. The only problem you have, like I told you, is the little matter of the finger on the button."

"Well, we've already solved that," Cray said.

"Then I might as well move out of here."

"Just give me a couple more minutes of your valuable time, Mr Roper ... Charlie..." Cray said. He sipped his cocktail, licked his lips and set the glass down. "How can I be sure that the flash drive will actually work?"

"You have my word on it," Roper said. "And you're certainly paying me enough."

"Indeed so. Half a million dollars in advance. And two million dollars now. However..." Cray paused and pursed his lips. "I still have one small worry on my mind."

Alex's leg had gone to sleep as he crouched, watching the scene from the stairs. Slowly he straightened it out. He wished he understood more of what they were saying. He knew that a flash drive was a type of storage device used in computer technology. But who or what was Milstar? And what was Eagle Strike?

"What's the problem?" Roper asked casually.

"I'm afraid *you* are, Mr Roper." The green eyes in Cray's round, babyish face were suddenly hard. "You are not as reliable as I had hoped. When you came to Paris, you were followed."

"That's not true."

"An English journalist found out about your gambling habit. He and a photographer followed you to la Tour d'Argent." Cray held up a hand to stop Roper interrupting. "I have dealt with them both. But you have disappointed me, Mr Roper. I wonder if I can still trust you."

"Now you listen to me, Damian." Roper spoke angrily. "We had a deal. I worked here with your technical boys. I gave them the information they needed to load the flash drive, and that's my part of it over. How you're going to get to the VIP lounge and how you'll actually activate the system ... that's your business. But you owe me two million dollars, and this journalist – whoever he was – doesn't make any difference at all."

"Blood money," Cray said.

"What?"

"That's what they call money paid to traitors."

"I'm no traitor!" Roper growled. "I needed the money, that's all. I haven't betrayed my country. So quit talking like this, pay me what you owe me and let me walk out of here."

"Of course I'm going to pay you what I owe you." Cray smiled. "You'll have to forgive me, Charlie. I was just thinking aloud." He gestured, his hand falling limply back. The American glanced round and Alex saw that there was an alcove to one side of the room. It was shaped like a giant bottle, with a curved wall behind and a curving glass door in front. Inside was a table, and on the table a leather attaché case.

"Your money is in there," Cray said.

"Thank you."

Neither Yassen Gregorovich nor the man with the spectacles had spoken throughout all this, but they watched intently as the American approached the alcove. There must have been some sort of sensor built into the door because it slid open automatically. Roper went up to the table and opened the case. Alex heard the two locks click up.

Then Roper turned round. "I hope this isn't your idea of a joke," he said. "This is empty."

Cray smiled at him from the sofa. "Don't worry," he said. "I'll fill it." He reached out and pressed a button on the coffee table in front of him. There was a hiss and the door of the alcove slid shut.

"Hey!" Roper shouted.

Cray pressed the button a second time.

For an instant nothing happened. Alex realized he was no longer breathing. His heart was beating at twice its normal rate. Then something bright and silver dropped down from somewhere high up inside the closed-off room, landing inside the case. Roper reached in and held up a small coin. It was a quarter – a twenty-five cent piece.

"Cray! What are you playing at?" he demanded.

More coins began to fall into the case. Alex couldn't see exactly what was happening but he guessed that the room really was like a bottle, totally sealed apart from a hole somewhere above. The coins were falling through the hole, the trickle rapidly turning into a cascade. In seconds the attaché case was full, and still the coins came, tumbling onto the pile, spreading out over the table and onto the floor.

Perhaps Charlie Roper had an inkling of what was about to happen. He forced his way through the shower of coins and pounded on the glass door. "Stop this!" he shouted. "Let me out of here!"

"But I haven't paid you all your money, Mr

Roper," Cray replied. "I thought you said I owed you two million dollars."

Suddenly the cascade became a torrent. Thousands and thousands of coins poured into the room. Roper cried out, bending an arm over his head, trying to protect himself. Alex quickly worked out the mathematics. Two million dollars, twenty-five cents at a time. The payment was being made in just about the smallest of small change. How many coins would there be? Already they filled all the available floor space, rising up to the American's knees. The torrent intensified. Now the rush of coins was solid and Roper's screams were almost drowned out by the clatter of metal against metal. Alex wanted to look away but he found himself fixated, his eyes wide with horror.

He could barely see the man any more. The coins thundered down. Roper was trying to swat them away, as if they were a swarm of bees. His arms and hands were vaguely visible but his face and body had disappeared. He lashed out with a fist and Alex saw a smear of blood appear on the door – but the toughened glass wouldn't break. The coins oozed forward, filling every inch of space. They rose up higher and higher. Roper was invisible now, sealed into the glittering mass.

If he was still screaming, nothing more could be heard.

And then, suddenly, it was over. The last coins fell. A grave of eight million quarters. Alex shuddered, trying to imagine what it must have been like to have been trapped inside. How had the American died? Had he been suffocated by the falling coins or crushed by their weight? Alex had no doubt that the man inside was dead. Blood money! Cray's sick joke couldn't have been more true.

Cray laughed.

"That was fun!" he said.

"Why did you kill him?" The man in the spectacles had spoken for the first time. He had a Dutch accent. His voice was trembling.

"Because he was careless, Henryk," Cray replied. "We can't make mistakes, not at this late stage. And it's not as if I broke any promises. I said I'd pay him two million dollars, and if you want to open the door and count it, two million dollars is exactly what you'll find."

"Don't open the door!" the man called Henryk gasped.

"No. I think it would be a bit messy." Cray smiled. "Well, we've taken care of Roper. We've got the flash drive. We're all set to go. So why don't we have another drink?"

Still crouching at the bottom of the stairs, Alex gritted his teeth, forcing himself not to panic. Every instinct told him to get up and run, but he knew he had to take care. What he had seen was almost beyond belief – but at least his mission was now clear. He had to get out of the compound, out of Sloterdijk, and back to England. Like it or not, he had to go back to MI6.

He knew now that he had been right all along and that Damian Cray was both mad and evil. All his posturing – his many charities and his speeches against violence – was precisely that; a facade. He was planning something that he called Eagle Strike, and whatever it was would take place in two days' time. It involved a security system and a VIP lounge. Was he going to break into an embassy? It didn't matter. Somehow he would make Alan Blunt and Mrs Jones believe him. There was a dead man called Charlie Roper. A connection with the National Security Agency of America. Surely Alex had enough information to persuade them to make an arrest.

But first he had to get out.

He turned just in time to see the figure looming above him. It was a guard, coming down the stairs. Alex started to react, but he was too late.

The guard had seen him. He was carrying a gun. Slowly Alex raised his hands. The guard gestured and Alex stood up, rising above the stair rail. On the other side of the room, Damian Cray saw him. His face lit up with delight.

"Alex Rider!" he exclaimed. "I was hoping to see *you* again. What a lovely surprise! Come on over and have a drink – and let me tell you how you're going to die."

PAIN SYNTHESIS

"Yassen has told me all about you," Cray said. "Apparently you worked for MI6. I have to say, that's a very novel idea. Are you still working for them now? Did they send you after me?"

Alex said nothing.

"If you don't answer my questions, I may have to start thinking about doing nasty things to you. Or getting Yassen to do them. That's what I pay him for. Pins and needles ... that sort of thing."

"MI6 don't know anything," Yassen said.

He and Cray were alone in the room with Alex. The guard and the man called Henryk had gone. Alex was sitting on the sofa with a glass of chocolate milk that Cray had insisted on pouring for him. Cray was now perched on the piano stool. His legs were crossed and he seemed completely relaxed as he sipped another cocktail.

"There's no way the intelligence services could know anything about us," Yassen went on. "And if they did, they wouldn't have sent Alex."

"Then why was he at the Pleasure Dome? Why is he here?" Cray turned to Alex. "I don't suppose you've come all this way to get my autograph. As a matter of fact, Alex, I'm rather pleased to see you. I was planning to come and find you one day anyway. You completely spoilt the launch of my Gameslayer. Much too clever by half! I was very cross with you, and although I'm rather busy at the moment, I was going to arrange a little accident..."

"Like you did for that woman in Hyde Park?" Alex asked.

"She was a nuisance. She asked impertinent questions. I hate journalists, and I hate smart-arse kids too. As I say, I'm very glad you managed to find your way here. It makes my life a lot easier."

"You can't do anything to me," Alex said. "MI6 know I'm here. They know all about Eagle Strike. You may have the codes, but you'll never be able to use them. And if I don't report in this evening, this whole place will be surrounded before tomorrow and you'll be in jail..."

Cray glanced at Yassen. The Russian shook his

head. "He's lying. He must have heard us talking from the stairs. He knows nothing."

Cray licked his lips. Alex realized that he was enjoying himself. He could see now just how crazy Cray was. The man didn't connect with the real world and Alex knew that whatever he was planning, it was going to be on a big scale – and probably lethal.

"It doesn't make any difference," Cray said. "Eagle Strike will have taken place in less than forty-eight hours from now. I agree with you, Yassen. This boy knows nothing. He's irrelevant. I can kill him and it won't make any difference at all."

"You don't have to kill him," Yassen said. Alex was surprised. The Russian had killed Ian Rider. He was Alex's worst enemy. But this was the second time Yassen had tried to protect him. "You can just lock him up until it's all over."

"You're right," Cray said. "I don't have to kill him. But I want to. It's something I want to do very much." He pushed himself off the piano stool and came over to Alex. "Do you remember I told you about pain synthesis?" he said. "In London. The demonstration... Pain synthesis allows game players to experience the hero's emotions – all his emotions, particularly those associated with pain and death. You may wonder how I programmed it into the software. The answer, my dear Alex, is by the use of volunteers such as yourself."

"I didn't volunteer," Alex muttered.

"Nor did the others. But they still helped me. Just as you will help me. And your reward will be an end to the pain. The comfort and the quiet of death..." Cray looked away. "You can take him," he said.

Two guards had come into the room. Alex hadn't heard them approach, but now they stepped out of the shadows and grabbed hold of him. He tried to fight back, but they were too strong for him. They pulled him off the sofa and away, down one of the passages leading from the room.

Alex managed to look back one last time. Cray had already forgotten him. He was holding the flash drive, admiring it. But Yassen was watching him and he looked worried. Then an automatic door shot down with a hiss of compressed air and Alex was dragged away, his feet sliding uselessly behind him, following the passageway to whatever it was that Damian Cray had arranged.

The cell was at the end of another underground corridor. The two guards threw Alex in, then waited as he turned round to face them. The one who had found him on the stairs spoke a few words with a heavy Dutch accent.

"The door closes and it stays closed. You find the way out. Or you starve."

That was it. The door slammed and Alex heard two bolts being drawn across. He heard the guards' footsteps fade into the distance. Suddenly everything was silent. He was on his own.

He looked around him. The cell was a bare metal box about five metres long and two metres wide with a single bunk, no water and no window. The door had closed flush to the wall. There was no crack round the side, not so much as a keyhole. He knew he had never been in worse trouble. Cray hadn't believed his story; he had barely even considered it. Whether Alex was with MI6 or not seemed to make no difference to him ... and the truth was that this time Alex really had got himself caught up in something without MI6 there to back him up. For once he had no gadgets to help him break out of the cell. He had brought the bicycle that Smithers had given him from London to Paris and then to Amsterdam. But right now it was parked outside Central Station in the city and would stay there until it was stolen or rusted away. Jack knew he had planned to break into the compound, but even if she did raise the alarm, how would anyone ever find him? Despair weighed down on him. He no longer had the strength to fight it.

And still he knew almost nothing. Why had Cray invested so much time and money in the game system he called Gameslayer? Why did he need the flash drive? What was the plane doing in the middle of the compound? Above all, what was Cray planning? Eagle Strike would take place in two days – but where, and what would it entail?

Alex forced himself to take control. He'd been locked up before. The important thing was to fight back – not to admit defeat. Cray had already made mistakes. Even speaking his own name on the phone when Alex called him from Saint-Pierre had been an error of judgement. He might have power, fame and enormous resources. He was certainly planning a huge operation. But he wasn't as clever as he thought. Alex could still beat him.

But how to begin? Cray had put him into this cell to experience what he called pain synthesis. Alex didn't like the sound of that. And what had the guard said? Find the way out – or starve. But there *was* no way out. Alex ran his hands across the walls. They were solid steel. He went over and examined the door a second time. Nothing.

It was tightly sealed. He glanced at the ceiling, at the single bulb burning behind a thick pane of glass. That only left the bunk...

He found the trapdoor underneath, built into the wall. It was like a cat flap, just big enough to take a human body. Gingerly, wondering if it might be booby-trapped, Alex reached out and pushed it. The metal flap swung inwards. There was some sort of tunnel on the other side, but he couldn't see anything. If he crawled into it, he would be entering a narrow space with no light at all – and he couldn't even be sure that the tunnel actually went anywhere. Did he have the courage to go in?

There was no alternative. Alex examined the cell one last time, knelt down and pushed himself forward. The metal flap swung open in front of him, then travelled down his back as he crawled into the tunnel. He felt it hit the back of his heels and there was a soft click. What was that? He couldn't see anything. He lifted a hand and waved it in front of his face. It was as if it wasn't there. He reached out in front of him and felt a solid wall. God! He had walked – crawled rather – into a trap. This wasn't the way out after all.

He pushed himself back the way he had come,

and that was when he discovered the flap was now locked. He kicked out with his feet but it wouldn't move. Panic, total and uncontrollable, overwhelmed him. He was buried alive, in total darkness, with no air. This was what Cray had meant by pain synthesis: a death too hideous to imagine.

Alex went mad.

Unable to control himself, he screamed out, his fists lashing against the walls of this metal coffin. He was suffocating.

His flailing hand hit a section of the wall and he felt it give way. There was a second flap! Gasping for air, he twisted round and into a second tunnel, as black and as chilling as the first. But at least there was some faint flicker of hope burning in his consciousness. There was a way through. If he could just keep a grip on himself, he might yet find his way back into the light.

The second tunnel was longer. Alex slithered forward, feeling the sheet metal under his hands. He forced himself to slow down. He was still completely blind. If there was a hole ahead of him, he would plunge into it before he knew what had happened. As he went, he tapped against the walls, searching for other passageways. His head knocked into something and he swore. The bad language helped him. It was good to direct his hatred against Damian Cray. And hearing his own voice reminded him he was still alive.

He had bumped into a ladder. He took hold of it with both hands and felt for the opening that must be above his shoulders. He was lying flat on his stomach, but slowly he manipulated himself round and began to climb up, feeling his way in case there was a ceiling overhead. His hand came into contact with something and he pushed. To his huge relief, light flooded in. He had opened some sort of trapdoor with a large, brightly lit room on the other side. Gratefully he climbed the last rungs and passed through.

The air was warm. Alex sucked it into his lungs, allowing his feelings of panic and claustrophobia to fade away. Then he looked up.

He was kneeling on a straw-covered floor in a room that was bathed in yellow light. Three of the walls seemed to have been built with huge blocks of stone. Blazing torches slanted in towards him, fixed to metal brackets. Gates at least ten metres high stood in front of him. They were made out of wood, with iron fastenings and a huge face carved into the surface. Some sort of Mexican god with saucer eyes and solid, block-like teeth. Alex had seen the face before but it took him a few moments to work out where. And then he knew exactly what lay ahead of him. He knew how Cray had programmed pain synthesis into his game.

The gates had appeared at the start of Feathered Serpent, the game that Alex had played in the Pleasure Dome in Hyde Park. Then it had been a computerized image, projected onto a screen – and Alex had been represented by an avatar, a two-dimensional version of himself. But Cray had also built an actual physical version of the game. Alex reached out and touched one of the walls. Sure enough, they weren't really stone but some sort of toughened plastic. The whole thing was like one of those walk-throughs at Disneyland … an ancient world reproduced with high-tech modern construction. There had been a time when Alex wouldn't have believed it possible, but he knew with a sick certainty that once the gates opened, he would find himself in a perfect reconstruction of the game – and that meant he would be facing the same challenges. Only this time it would be for real: real flames, real acid, real spears and – if he made a mistake – real death.

Cray had told him that he had used other "volunteers". Presumably they had been filmed fighting their way through the various challenges;

and all the time their emotions had been recorded and then somehow digitally transferred and programmed into the Gameslayer system. It was sick. Alex realized that the darkness of the underground passages hadn't even been part of the real challenge. That began now.

He didn't move. He needed time to think, to remember as much as he could about the game he had played at the Pleasure Dome. There had been five zones. First some sort of temple, with a crossbow and a sword concealed in the walls. Would Cray provide him with weapons in this reconstruction? He would have to wait and see. What came after the temple? There had been a pit with a flying creature: half butterfly, half dragon. After that Alex had run down a corridor – spears shooting out of the walls – and into a jungle, the home of the metallic snakes. Then there had been a mirror maze guarded by Aztec gods and finally a pool of fire, his exit to the next level.

A pool of fire. If that was reproduced here, it would kill him. Alex remembered what Cray had said. *The comfort and the quiet of death*. There was no way out of this madhouse. If he did manage to survive the five zones, he would be allowed to finish it by throwing himself into the flames.

Alex felt hatred well up inside him. He could actually taste it. Damian Cray was beyond evil.

What could he do? There would be no way back through the tunnels and Alex wasn't sure he had the nerve even to try. He had only one choice, and that was to continue. He had almost beaten the game once. That at least gave him a little hope. On the other hand, there was a world of difference between manipulating a controller and actually attempting the action himself. He couldn't move or react with the speed of an electronic figure. Nor would he be given extra lives. If he was killed once, he would stay dead.

He stood up. At once the gates swung silently open, and there ahead of him was the temple that he had last seen in the game. He wondered if his progress was being monitored. Could he at least rely on an element of surprise?

He walked through the gates. The temple was exactly how he remembered it from the screen at the Pleasure Dome: a vast space with stone walls covered in strange carvings and pillars, statues crouching at their base, stretching far above him. Even the stained-glass windows had been reproduced with images of UFOs hovering over fields of golden corn. And there too were the cameras, swivelling to follow him and, presumably, to record whatever progress he made. Organ music, modern rather than religious, throbbed all around him. Alex shivered, barely able to accept that this was really happening.

He walked further into the temple, every sense alert, waiting for an attack that he knew could come from any direction. He wished now that he had played Feathered Serpent more carefully. He had raced through the zones at such speed that he had probably missed half of the ambushes. His feet rang out on the silver floor. Ahead of him, rusting staircases that reminded him of a submarine or a submerged ship twisted upwards. He thought of trying one of them. But he hadn't gone that way when he was playing the game and preferred not to now. It was better to stick with what he knew.

The alcove that contained the crossbow was underneath a wooden pulpit, carved in the shape of a dragon. It was almost completely covered by what looked like green ivy – but Alex knew that the twisting vines carried an electrical charge. He could see the weapon resting against the stonework, and there was just enough of a gap. Was it worth the risk? Alex tensed himself, preparing to reach in, then threw himself full length on the floor. Half a second later and it would have

been fatal. He had remembered the razor boomerang at the same instant that he had heard a
whistling sound coming from nowhere. He had
no time to prepare himself. He hit the ground so
hard that the breath was driven out of him. There
was a flash and a series of sparks. He felt a burning pain across his shoulders and knew that he
hadn't been quite fast enough. The boomerang
had sliced open his T-shirt, also cutting his skin.
It had been a close thing. Any closer and he
wouldn't even have made it into the second zone.

And silently the cameras watched. Everything
was being recorded. One day it would be fed into
Cray's software – presumably Feathered Serpent 2.

Alex sat up and tried to pull his torn shirt
together. At least the boomerang had helped in
one way. It had hit the ivy, cutting and short-
circuiting the electric wires. Alex stretched an
arm into the alcove and took out the crossbow.
It was antique – wood and iron – but it seemed
to be working. Even so, Cray had cheated him.
There was an arrow in it, but it had no point. It
was too blunt to damage anything.

He decided to take both the crossbow and the
arrow with him anyway. He moved away from the
alcove and over to the wall where he knew he
would find the sword. It was about twenty metres

above him but there were loose stones and hand-holds indicating a way up. Alex was about to start climbing but then he had second thoughts. He had already had one close escape. The wall would almost certainly be booby-trapped. He would be halfway up and a stone would come loose. If he fell, he would break a leg. Cray would enjoy that, watching him lie helpless on the silver floor until some other missile was fired into him to finish him off. And anyway, the sword would probably have no blade.

But thinking about it, Alex suddenly realized that he had the answer. He knew how to beat the simulated world that Cray had built.

Every computer game is a series of programmed events, with nothing random, nothing left to chance. When Alex had played the game in the Pleasure Dome, he had collected the crossbow and then used it to shoot the creature that had attacked him. In the same way, locked doors would have keys; poisons would have antidotes. No matter how much choice you might seem to have, you were always obeying a hidden set of rules.

But Alex had not been programmed. He was a human being and he could do what he wanted. It had cost him a torn shirt and a very narrow escape – but he had learnt his lesson. If he hadn't tried to get the crossbow, he wouldn't have made himself a target for the boomerang. Climbing up the wall to get the sword would put him in danger because he would be doing exactly what was expected.

To get out of the world that Cray had built for him, he had to do everything that *wasn't* expected.

In other words he had to cheat.

And he would start right now.

He went over to one of the blazing torches and tried to remove it from the wall. He wasn't surprised to find that the whole thing was bolted into place. Cray had thought of everything. But even if he controlled the holders, he couldn't control the flames themselves. Alex pulled off his shirt and wrapped it round the end of the wooden arrow. Then he set it on fire. He smiled to himself. Now he had a weapon that hadn't been programmed.

The exit door was at the far end of the temple. Alex was supposed to take a direct path to it. Instead, he went the long way round, staying close to the walls, avoiding any traps that might be lying in wait. Ahead of him he could see the second chamber – the rain-drenched pit with its pillars rising from the depths below and ending at floor level. He passed through the door and stopped on a narrow ledge; the tops of the pillars – barely bigger than soup plates – offered him a path of stepping stones across the void. Alex remembered the flying creature that had attacked him. He looked up. Yes, there it was, almost lost in the gloom: a nylon wire running from the opposite side to the door above his head. He thrust upwards with the burning arrow, holding the flame against the wire.

It worked. The wire caught fire and then snapped. Cray had built a robotic version of the creature that had attacked him in the game. Alex knew that it would have swooped down when he was halfway across, rushing into him and knocking him off his perch, causing him to plunge into whatever lay below. Now he watched with quiet satisfaction as the creature tumbled down from the ceiling and dangled in front of him, a jumble of metal and feathers that was more like a dead parrot than a mythical monster.

The way ahead was clear but the rain was still falling, splashing down from some hidden sprinkler system. The stepping stones would be slippery. Alex knew that his avatar would have been unable to remove its shoes for better grip. He quickly slipped off his trainers, tied them together and hung them round his neck. His socks went into his pocket. Then he jumped. The trick, he knew, was to do this quickly: not to stop, not to look down. He took a breath, then started. The rain blinded him. The tops of the pillars were only just big enough to contain his bare feet. On the very last one he lost his balance. But he didn't have to use his feet – he could move in a way that his avatar couldn't. He threw himself forward, stretching out his hands and allowing his own momentum to carry him towards safety. His chest hit the ground and he clung on, dragging his legs over the edge of the pit. He had made it to the other side.

A corridor ran off to the left, the walls close together and decorated with hideous Aztec faces. Alex remembered how his avatar had run through here, dodging between a hail of wooden spears. He glanced down and saw that there was what looked like a smoking stream in the floor.

Acid! What now?

He needed another weapon and he had an idea how to get one. He took out his socks, rolled them into a ball and threw them down the corridor. As he had hoped, the movement was enough to activate the sensors that controlled the hidden guns. Short wooden spears spat out of the lips of the Aztec gods at fantastic speed, striking the opposite walls. One of the spears broke in half. Alex picked it up and felt the needle-sharp point. It was exactly what he wanted. He tucked it into the belt of his trousers. He still had the crossbow; now he had a bolt that might fit it too.

The computer game had been programmed so that there was only one way forward. Alex had been able to dodge both the spears and the acid river easily enough when he was playing Feathered Serpent. But he knew he would be unable to do the same in this grotesque three-dimensional version. He would only have to take one false step and he would be finished. He could imagine splashing into the acid and then panicking. He would be driven straight into the path of the spears as he tried to reach the next zone. No. There had to be another way.

Alex forced himself to concentrate. Ignore the rules! He turned the three words over and over in his mind. Moving along the corridor wasn't an option. But how about up? He put on his shoes, then took a tentative step. The spears nearest the entrance had already been fired. He was safe so long as he didn't move too far down the corridor. He grabbed hold of the wall and, balancing the crossbow over his shoulder, began to climb. The

Aztec heads made perfect footholds, and only when he was at the very top did he begin to make his way along, high above the floor and away from danger. One step at a time, he edged forward. He came to a camera mounted in the ceiling and, with a smile, wrenched out the wire. There was a lot of it and he decided to keep that too.

He reached the end of the corridor and climbed down into the fourth zone, the jungle. He was surprised to discover that the vegetation pressing in on him from all sides was real. He had expected plastic and paper. He could feel the heat in the air and the ground underfoot was soft and wet. What traps were waiting for him here? He remembered the robotic snakes that had barely managed to get close when he played the game, and searched warily for the tracks that would propel something similar his way.

There were no tracks. Alex took another step forward and stopped, paralysed by the horror of what he saw.

There was a snake, and, like the leaves and the creepers, it was real. It was as thick as a man's waist and at least five metres long, lying motionless in a patch of long grass. Its eyes were two black diamonds. For a brief second, Alex hoped it might be dead. But then its tongue flickered out and the whole body heaved, and he knew that he was facing a living thing – one that was beyond nightmares.

The snake had been encased in a fantastic body suit. Alex had no idea how long it could have survived wrapped up like this. As terrifying as the creature was, he still felt a spark of pity for it, seeing what had been done. The suit was made out of wire that had been twisted round and round the full length of the animal, with vicious spikes and razors welded on from the neck all the way to the tail. Looking past the tail, Alex could see dozens of lines cut into the soft ground. Whatever the snake touched, it sliced. It couldn't help itself. And it was slithering towards him.

He couldn't have moved if he had wanted to, but something told him that keeping still was the only chance he had. The snake had to be some sort of boa constrictor, part of the Boidae family. A useless piece of information he had picked up in biology class suddenly came back to him. The snake ate mainly birds and monkeys, finding its victims by smell, then coiling round and suffocating them. But Alex knew that if the snake attacked him, this wouldn't be how he would die. The razors and spikes would cut him to pieces.

And it was getting closer. Wave after wave

of glinting silver rippled behind it as it dragged the razors along. Now it was just a metre away. Moving very slowly, Alex lowered the crossbow from his shoulder. He pulled the wire back to load it, then reached into the waistband of his trousers. The broken spear was still there. Trying not to give the snake any reason to attack him, Alex fixed the length of wood into the stock. He was lucky. The spear was exactly the right length.

He wasn't meant to have a weapon in this zone. That hadn't been part of the program. But despite everything Cray had thrown at him he still had the crossbow and now it was loaded.

Alex cried out. He couldn't help himself. The snake had suddenly jerked forward, dragging itself over his trainer. The razors cut into the soft material, only millimetres away from his foot. He instinctively kicked out. At once the snake reared back. Alex saw black flames ignite in its eyes. Its tongue flickered. It was about to launch itself at him. He brought the crossbow round and fired. There was nothing else he could do. The bolt entered the snake's mouth and continued out of the back of its head. Alex leapt back, avoiding the deadly convulsions of the creature's body. The snake thrashed and twisted, cutting the grass and the nearby bushes to shreds. Then it lay still.

Alex knew that he had killed it, and he wasn't sorry. What had been done to the snake was revolting. He was glad he had put it out of its misery.

There was one more zone left – the mirror maze. Alex knew that there would be Aztec gods waiting for him. Probably guards in fancy dress. Even if he got past them, he would only find himself facing the pool of fire. But he'd had enough. To hell with Damian Cray. He looked up. He had disabled one of the security cameras and there weren't any others in view. He had found a blind spot in this insane playground. That suited him perfectly.

It was time to find his own way out.

THE TRUTH ABOUT ALEX

There are no gods crueller or more ferocious than those of the Aztecs. That was the reason why Damian Cray had chosen them to inhabit his computer game.

He had summoned three of them to patrol the mirror maze, the fifth and last zone in the huge arena he had built beneath the compound. Tlaloc, the god of rain, was half human, half alligator, with jagged teeth, claw-like hands and a thick scaly tail that dragged behind him. Xipe Totec, the lord of spring, had torn out his own eyes. They were still dangling in front of his gruesome, pain-distorted face. And Xolotl, bringer of fire, walked on feet that had been smashed and wrenched round to face backwards. Flames leapt out of his hands, reflected a hundred times in the mirrors and adding to the twisting clouds of smoke.

Of course, there was nothing supernatural about the three creatures waiting for Alex to appear. Beneath the grotesque masks, the plastic skin and make-up, they were nothing more than criminals, recently released from Bijlmer, the largest prison in the Netherlands. They now worked as guards for Cray Software Technology, but they had special duties too. This was one of them. The three men were armed with curved swords, javelins, steel claws and flame-throwers. They were looking forward to using them.

It was the one dressed as Xolotl who saw Alex first.

The camera in zone three had gone down, so there had been no way of knowing if Alex was on his way or if the snake had finished him. But suddenly there was a movement. The guard saw a figure lurch round a corner, naked to the waist. The boy was making no attempt to hide, and the guard saw why.

Alex Rider was soaked in blood. His entire chest was bright red. His mouth was opening and closing, but no sound came out. Then the guard saw the wooden spear sticking out of his chest. The boy had obviously tried to run down the corridor but hadn't quite made it. One of the spears had found its target.

Alex saw the guard and stopped. He dropped to his knees. One hand pointed limply at the spear, then fell. He looked upwards and tried to speak. More blood trickled out of his mouth. His eyes closed and he pitched to one side. He didn't move again.

The guard relaxed. The boy's death meant nothing to him. He reached into the pocket of his chain-mail shirt and took out a radio transmitter.

"It's over," he said, speaking in Dutch. "The boy's been killed by a spear."

Neon strips flickered on throughout the game zone. In the harsh white light the different zones seemed cruder, more like fairground attractions. The guards, too, looked ridiculous in their fancy dress. The dangling eyes were painted ping-pong balls. The alligator body was nothing more than a rubber suit. The backward-facing feet could have come out of a joke shop. The three of them formed a circle around Alex.

"He's still breathing," one of them said.

"Not for much longer." The second guard glanced at the point of the spear, covered in rapidly congealing blood.

"What shall we do with him?"

"Leave him here. It's not our job. Disposal can pick him up later."

They walked away. One of them stopped beside a wall, painted to look like crumbling stone, and pulled open a concealed panel to reveal a button. He pressed it and the wall slid open. There was a brightly lit corridor on the other side. The three men went off to change.

Alex opened his eyes.

The trick he had played was so old that he was almost ashamed. If it had been done on the stage, it wouldn't have fooled a six-year-old. But he supposed that circumstances were a little different here.

Left on his own in the miniature jungle, he had reclaimed the broken spear that he had used to kill the snake. He had tied it to his chest using the wire he had torn out of the security camera. Then he had covered himself with blood taken from the dead snake. That had been the worst part, but he'd had to make sure that the illusion would work. Steeling himself, he had scooped up some more of the blood and put it in his mouth. He could still taste it now and he was having to force himself not to swallow. But it had fooled the men completely. None of them had looked too closely. They had seen what they wanted to see.

Alex waited until he was certain he was alone, then sat up and untied the spear. He would just have to hope that the cameras had all been turned off when the game had ended. The exit was still open and Alex stole through, leaving the make-believe world behind him. He found himself in an ordinary corridor, stretching into the distance with tiled walls and plain wooden doors on either side. He knew that although the immediate danger was behind him, he could hardly afford to start relaxing yet. He was half naked and covered in blood. He was still trapped in the heart of the compound. And it could only be a matter of time before someone discovered that the body had disappeared and realized the trick that had been played.

He opened the first of the doors. It led into a storage cupboard. The second and third doors were locked, but halfway down the corridor he found a changing room with showers, lockers and a laundry basket. Alex knew that it would cost him precious minutes, but he had to get clean. He stripped and showered, then dried himself and got dressed again. Before he left the room he searched through the laundry basket and found a shirt to replace the one he had burnt. The shirt was dirty and two sizes too big, but he pulled it on gratefully.

Carefully he opened the door – and quickly closed it again as two men walked past, talking in Dutch. They seemed to be heading for the mirror maze, and Alex hoped they weren't part of the disposal team. If so, the alarm would be raised at any moment. He counted the seconds until they had gone, then crept out and hurried the other way.

He came to a staircase. He had no idea where it went, but he was certain he had to go up.

The stairs led to a circular area with several corridors leading off it. There were no windows. The only illumination came from industrial lights set at intervals in the ceiling. He looked at his watch. It was eleven fifteen. Two and a quarter hours had passed since he had first broken into the compound; it felt much longer. He thought about Jack, waiting for him in the hotel in Amsterdam. She would be out of her mind with worry.

Everything was silent. Alex guessed that most of Cray's people would be asleep. He chose a corridor and followed it to another staircase. Again he went up, and found himself in a room that he knew. Cray's study. The room where he had seen the man called Charlie Roper die.

Alex was almost afraid to go in. But the room was deserted and, peering through the opening, he could see that the bottle-shaped chamber had been cleared, the money and the body taken away. It seemed strange to him that there should be no guard assigned to this room, at the very heart of Cray's network. But then again, why should there be? All the security was centred on the main gate. Alex was supposedly dead. Cray had nothing to fear.

Ahead of him was the staircase that he knew would lead up to the glass cube and out onto the square. But as tempted as he was to race over to it, Alex realized he would never have another opportunity like this. Somewhere in the back of his mind, he knew that even if he made it to MI6, he still had no real proof that Cray wasn't just the pop celebrity and businessman that everyone thought. Alan Blunt and Mrs Jones hadn't believed him the last time he'd seen them. They might not believe him again.

Ignoring his first instincts, Alex went over to the desk. There were about a dozen framed photographs on the surface, each and every one showing a picture of Damian Cray. Ignoring them, Alex turned his attention to the drawers. They were unlocked. The lower drawers contained dozens of different documents but most of them were nothing more than lists of figures and hardly looked promising. Then he came to the last drawer and let out a gasp of disbelief. The metallic capsule that Cray had been holding when he talked to the American was simply sitting there. Alex picked it up and weighed it in the palm of his hand. The flash drive. It contained computer codes. Its job was to break through some sort of security system. It had come with a price tag of two and a half million dollars. It had cost Roper his life.

And Alex had it! He wanted to examine it, but he could do that later. He slipped it into his trouser pocket and hurried over to the stairs.

Ten minutes later the alarms sounded throughout the compound. The two men that Alex had seen had indeed gone into the mirror maze to pick up the body and discovered that it wasn't there. They should have raised the alarm at once, but there had been a delay. The men had assumed that one of the other teams must have collected it and had gone to find them. It was only when they discovered the dead snake and the spear with the coil of wire that they put together what had taken place.

While this was happening, a van was driving out of the compound. Neither the tired guards at the gate nor the driver had noticed the figure lying flat, spreadeagled on the roof. But why should they? The van was leaving, not arriving. It didn't even stop in front of the security cameras. The guard merely checked the driver's ID and opened the gate. The alarm rang seconds after the van had passed through.

There was a system in place at Cray Software Technology. Nobody was allowed to enter or leave during a security alert. Every van was equipped with a two-way radio and the guard at the gate immediately signalled to the driver and told him to return. The driver stopped before he had even reached the traffic light and wearily obeyed. But it was already too late.

Alex slipped off the roof and dropped to the ground. Then he ran off into the night.

Damian Cray was back in his office, sitting on the sofa holding a glass of milk. He had been in bed when the alarm went off and now he was wearing a silver dressing gown, dark blue pyjamas and soft cotton slippers. Something bad had happened to his face. The life had drained out of it, leaving behind a cold, empty mask that could have been cut out of glass. A single vein throbbed above one of his glazed eyes.

Cray had just discovered that the flash drive had been taken from his desk. He had searched all the drawers, ripping them out, upturning them and scattering their contents across the floor. Then, with an inarticulate howl of rage, he had thrown himself onto the desktop, flailing about with his arms and sending telephones, files and photograph frames flying. He had smashed a paperweight into his computer screen, shattering the glass. And then he had sat down on the sofa and called for a glass of milk.

Yassen Gregorovich had watched all this without speaking. He too had been called from his room by the alarm bells, but, unlike Cray, he hadn't been asleep. Yassen never slept for more than four hours. The night was too valuable. He might go for a run or work out in the gym. He might listen to classical music. On this night he had been working with a tape recorder and a well-thumbed exercise book. He was teaching himself Japanese, one of the nine languages he had made it his business to learn.

Yassen had heard the alarms and known instinctively that Alex Rider had escaped. He had turned off the tape recorder. And he had smiled.

Now he waited for Cray to break the silence. It had been Yassen who had suggested quietly that Cray should look for the flash drive. He wondered if he would get the blame for the theft.

"He was meant to be dead!" Cray moaned. "They told me he was dead!" He glanced at Yassen, suddenly angry. "You knew he'd been in here."

"I suspected it," Yassen said.

"Why?"

Yassen considered. "Because he's Alex," he said simply.

"Then tell me about him!"

"There is only so much I can tell you." Yassen stared into the distance. His face gave nothing away. "The truth about Alex is that there is not a boy in the world like him," he began, speaking slowly and softly. "Consider for a moment. Tonight you tried to kill him – and not just simply with a bullet or a knife, but in a way that should have terrified him. He escaped and he found his way here. He must have seen the stairs. Any other boy – any man even – would have climbed them instantly. His only desire would have been to get out of here. But not Alex. He stopped; he searched. That is what makes him unique, and that is why he is so valuable to MI6."

"How did he find his way here?"

"I don't know. If you'd allowed me to question him before you sent him into that game of yours, I might have been able to find out."

"This is not my fault, Mr Gregorovich! You should have killed him in the South of France when you had the chance." Cray drank the milk and set the glass down. He had a white moustache on his upper lip. "Why didn't you?" he demanded.

"I tried..."

"That nonsense in the bullring! That was stupid. I think you knew he'd escape."

"I hoped he might," Yassen agreed. He was beginning to get bored with Cray. He didn't like being asked to explain himself, and when he spoke again it was almost as much for his own benefit as Cray's. "I knew him..." he said.

"You mean ... before Saint-Pierre?"

"I met him once. But even then ... I knew him already. The moment I saw him, I knew who he was and what he was. The image of his father..." Yassen stopped himself. He had already said more than he had meant to. "He knows nothing of this," he muttered. "No one has ever told him the truth."

But Cray was no longer interested. "I can't do

anything without the flash drive," he moaned, and suddenly there were tears brimming in his eyes. "It's all over! Eagle Strike! All the planning. Years and years of it. Millions of pounds. And it's all *your* fault!"

So there it was at last, the finger of blame.

For a few seconds, Yassen Gregorovich was seriously tempted to kill Damian Cray. It would be very quick: a three-finger strike into the pale, flabby throat. Yassen had worked for many evil people – not that he ever thought of them in terms of good and evil. All that mattered to him was how much they were prepared to pay. Some of them – Herod Sayle, for example – had planned to kill millions of people. The numbers were irrelevant to Yassen. People died all the time. He knew that every time he drew a breath, at that exact moment, somewhere in the world a hundred or a thousand people would be taking their last. Death was everywhere; it could not be measured.

But recently something inside him had changed. Perhaps it was meeting Alex again that had done it; perhaps it was his age. Although Yassen looked as if he was in his late twenties, he was in fact thirty-five. He was getting old. Too old, anyway, for his line of work. He was beginning to think it might be time to stop.

And that was why he now decided not to murder Damian Cray. Eagle Strike was only two days away. It would make him richer than he could have dreamt and it would allow him to return, at last, to his homeland, Russia. He would buy a house in St Petersburg and live comfortably, perhaps doing occasional business with the Russian mafia. The city was teeming with criminal activity and for a man with his wealth and experience, anything would be possible.

Yassen stretched out a hand, the same hand he would have used to strike his employer down. "You worry too much," he said. "For all we know, Alex may still be in the compound. But even if he has made it through the gate, he can't have gone far. He has to get out of Sloterdijk and back to Amsterdam. I have already instructed every man we have to get out there and find him. If he tries to get into the city, he will be intercepted."

"How do you know he's going into the city?" Cray demanded.

"It's the middle of the night. Where else could he go?" Yassen stood up and yawned. "Alex Rider will be back here before sunrise and you will have your flash drive."

"Good." Cray looked at the wreckage scattered across the floor. "And next time I get my hands on him I'll make sure he doesn't walk away. Next time I'll deal with him myself."

Yassen said nothing. Turning his back on Damian Cray, he walked slowly out of the room.

PEDAL POWER

The local train pulled into Amsterdam's Central Station and began to slow down. Alex was sitting on his own, his face resting against the window, barely conscious of the long, empty platforms or the great canopy stretching over his head. It was around midnight and he was exhausted. He knew Jack would be frantic, waiting for him at the hotel. He was eager to see her. He suddenly felt a need to be looked after. He just wanted a hot bath, a hot chocolate ... and bed.

The first time he had gone out to Sloterdijk, he had cycled both ways. But the second time, he had saved his energy and left the bike at the station. The journey back was short but he was enjoying it, knowing that every second put Cray and his compound a few more metres behind him.

He also needed the time to think about what he had just been through, to try to understand what it all meant. A plane that burst into flames. A VIP lounge. Something called Milstar. The man with the pock-marked face...

And he still had no answer to the biggest question of all. Why was Cray doing all this? He was massively rich. He had fans all over the world. Only a few days ago he had been shaking hands with the president of the United States. His music was still played on the radio and his every appearance drew massive crowds. The Gameslayer system would make him another fortune. If ever there was a man who had no need to conspire and to kill, it was him.

Eagle Strike.

What did the two words mean?

The train came to a halt; the doors hissed open. Alex checked that the flash drive was still in his pocket and got out.

There was barely anyone around on the platform but the main ticket hall was more crowded. Students and other young travellers were arriving on the international lines. Some of them were slumped on the floor, leaning against oversized rucksacks. They all looked spaced out in the hard, artificial light. Alex guessed it would take him about ten minutes to cycle down to the hotel on the Herengracht. If he was awake enough to remember where it was.

He passed through the heavy glass doors and found his bike where he had left it, chained to some railings. He had just unlocked it when he stopped, sensing the danger before he even saw it. This was something he had never learnt. Even his uncle, who had spent years training him to be a spy, would have been unable to explain it; the instinct that now told him he had to move – and fast. He looked around him. There was a wide cobbled area leading down to an expanse of water, with the city beyond. A kiosk selling hot dogs was still open. Sausages were turning over a burner but there was no sign of the vendor. A few couples were strolling across the bridges over the canals, enjoying a night that had become warm and dry. The sky wasn't black so much as a deep midnight blue.

Somewhere a clock struck the hour, the chimes echoing across the city.

Alex noticed a car, parked so that it faced the station. Its headlamps blinked on, throwing a beam of light across the square towards him. A moment later a second car did the same. Then a third. All three cars were the same: two-seater

Smart cars. More lights came on. There were six vehicles parked in a semicircle around him, covering every angle of the station square. They were all black. With their short bodies and slightly bulbous driving compartments, they looked almost like toys. But Alex knew with a feeling of cold certainty that they weren't here for fun.

Doors swung open. Men stepped out, turned into black silhouettes by their own headlamps. For a split second nobody moved. They had him. There was nowhere for him to go.

Alex stretched out his left thumb, moving it towards the bell that still looked ridiculous, attached to the handlebar of his bike. There was a small silver lever sticking out. Pushing it would ring the bell. Alex pulled. The top of the bell sprang open to reveal five buttons inside, each one a different colour. Smithers had described them in the manual. They were colour-coded for ease of use. Now it was time to find out if they worked.

As if sensing that something was about to happen, the black shadows had begun to move across the square. Alex pressed the orange button and felt the shudder beneath his hands as two tiny heat-seeking missiles exploded out of the ends of the handlebars. Trailing orange flames, they shot across the square. Alex saw the men stop, uncertain. The missiles soared into the air, then curved back, their movement perfectly synchronized. As Alex had suspected, the hottest thing in the square was the grill in the hot-dog kiosk. The missiles fell on it, both striking at exactly the same time. There was a huge explosion, a fireball of flame that spread across the cobbles and was reflected in the water of the canal. Burning fragments of wood and pieces of sausage rained down. The blast hadn't been strong enough to kill anyone, but it had created the perfect diversion. Alex grabbed the bike and dragged it back into the station. The square was blocked. This was the only way.

But even as he re-entered the ticket hall, he saw other men running across the concourse towards him. At this time of night the crowds were moving slowly. Anyone running had to have a special reason, and Alex knew for certain that the reason was him. Cray's men must have been in radio contact with each other. Now that one group had spotted him, they would all know where he was.

He jumped on the bike and pedalled along the flat stone floor as fast as he could: past the ticket booths, the newspaper kiosks, the information

boards and the ramps leading up to the platforms, trying to put as much space as he could
between himself and his pursuers. A woman
pushing a motorized cleaning machine stepped in
front of him and he had to swerve, almost knocking over a bearded man with a vast rucksack. The
man swore at him in German. Alex raced on.

There was a door at the very end of the main
hall, but before he could reach it, it burst open
and more men came running in, blocking his way.
Pedalling furiously, Alex spun the bike round and
headed for the one way out of this nightmare.
An empty escalator, going down. Before he even
knew what he was doing, he had launched himself onto the metal treads and was bouncing and
shuddering head first into the ground. He was
thrown from side to side, his body slamming
against the steel panels. He wondered if the front
wheel would crumple with the strain or if the
tyres would puncture against the sharp edges.
But then he had reached the bottom and he was
riding – bizarrely – through a subway station,
with ticket windows on one side and automatic
gates on the other. He was glad it was so late.
The station was almost empty. But still a few
heads turned in astonishment as he entered a
long passageway and disappeared from sight.

It was definitely the wrong time for this, but even so Alex found himself admiring the Bad Boy's handling ability. The aluminium frame was light and manageable but the solid down tube kept the bike stable. He came to a corner and automatically went into attack position. He pressed down on the outside pedal and put his weight on it, at the same time keeping his body low. His entire centre of gravity was focused on the point where the tyres came into contact with the ground, and the bike took the corner with total control. This was something Alex had learnt years ago, mountain biking in the Pennines. He had never expected to use the same techniques in a subway station under Amsterdam!

A second escalator brought him back up to street level and Alex found himself on the other side of the square, away from the station. The remains of the hot-dog kiosk were still burning. A police car had arrived and he could see the hysterical hot-dog salesman trying to explain what had happened to an officer. For a moment he hoped he would be able to slip away unnoticed. But then he heard the screech of tyres as one of the Smart cars skidded backwards in an arc and then shot forward in his direction. They had seen him! And they were after him again.

He began to pedal down the Damrak, one of the main streets in Amsterdam, quickly picking up speed. He glanced back. A second Smart car had joined the first, and with a sinking heart he knew that his legs would be no match for their engines. He had perhaps twenty seconds before they caught up with him.

Then a bell clanged and there was a loud metallic clattering. A tram was coming towards him, thundering along the tracks on its way to the station. Alex knew what he had to do. He could hear the Smart cars coming up behind him. The tram was a great metal box, filling his vision ahead. At the very last moment, he twisted the handlebars, throwing himself directly in front of the tram. He saw the driver's horrified face, felt the bicycle wheels shudder as they crossed the tracks. But then he was on the other side and the tram had become a wall that would – at least for a few seconds – separate him from the Smart cars.

Even so, one of them tried to follow. It was a terrible mistake. The car was halfway across the tracks when the tram hit it. There was a huge crash and the car spun away into the night. It was followed by a terrible grinding and metallic screaming as the tram derailed. The tram's second carriage whipped round and hit the other Smart car, batting it away like a fly. As Alex pedalled away from the Damrak, across a pretty, white-painted bridge, he left behind him a scene of total devastation, the first police sirens cutting through the air.

He found himself cycling through a series of narrow streets that were more crowded, with people drifting in and out of pornographic cinemas and striptease clubs. He had accidentally drifted into the famous red-light district of Amsterdam. He wondered what Jack would make of that. A woman standing in a doorway winked at him. Alex ignored her and rode on.

There were three black motorbikes at the end of the street.

Alex groaned. They were 400cc Suzuki Bandits and there could only be one reason why they were there, silent and unmoving. They were waiting for him. The moment their riders saw him, they kick-started their engines. Alex knew he had to get away – and fast. He looked around.

On one side of him dozens of people were streaming in and out of a parade of neon-lit shops. On the other a narrow canal stretched into the distance, with darkness and possible safety on the other side. But how was he going to get across? There wasn't a bridge in sight.

But perhaps there was a way. A boat was turning. It was one of the famous glass-topped cruisers, sitting low in the water and carrying tourists on a late-night dinner cruise. It had swung diagonally across the water so that it was almost touching both banks. The captain had misjudged the angle, and the boat seemed to be jammed.

Alex propelled himself forward. Simultaneously he pressed the green button under the bicycle bell. There was a water bottle suspended upside down under his saddle and out of the corner of his eye he saw a silver-grey liquid squirt out onto the road. He was hurtling towards the canal, leaving a snail-like trail behind him. He heard the roar of the Suzuki motorbikes and knew that they had caught up with him. Then everything happened at once.

Alex left the road, crossed the pavement and forced the bike up into the air. The first of the motorbikes reached the section of road that was covered with the ooze. At once the driver lost control, skidding so violently that he almost seemed to be throwing himself off on purpose. His bike smashed into a second bike, bringing that one down too. At the same time, Alex came hurtling down onto the reinforced glass roof of the tourist boat and began to pedal its full length. He could see diners gazing up at him in astonishment. A waiter with a tray of glasses spun round, dropping everything. There was the flash of a camera. Then he had reached the other side. Carried by his own momentum, he soared off the roof, over a line of bollards, and came to a skidding halt on the opposite bank of the canal.

He looked back – just in time to see that the third Bandit had managed to follow him. It was already in the air and the diners on the boat were gazing up in alarm as it descended towards them. They were right to be scared. The motorbike was too heavy. It crashed onto the glass roof, which shattered beneath it. Bike and rider disappeared into the cabin as the tourists, screaming, threw themselves out of the way. Plates and tables exploded; the lights in the cabin fused and went out. Alex didn't have time to see more.

He wasn't going to be able to hide in the darkness after all. Another pair of Bandits had found him, roaring up the side of the canal towards him. Pedalling frantically, he tried to get out of sight, turning into one road, cutting down another, around a corner, across a square. His legs and thighs were on fire. He knew he couldn't go on much further.

And then he made his mistake.

It was an alleyway, dark and inviting. It would lead him somewhere he wouldn't be found. That was what he thought. But he was only halfway down it when a man suddenly stepped out in front of him, holding a machine gun. Behind him the two Bandits edged closer, cutting off the way back.

The man with the machine gun took aim. Alex's finger stabbed down, this time finding the yellow button. At once there was an explosion of brilliant white light as the magnesium flare concealed inside the Digital Evolution headlight ignited. Alex couldn't believe how much light was pouring out of the bike. The whole area was illuminated. The man with the machine gun was completely blinded.

Alex hit the blue button. There was a loud hiss. Somewhere under his legs a cloud of blue smoke poured out of the air pump connected to the bicycle frame. The two Bandits had been chasing up behind him, and they now plunged into the smoke and disappeared.

Everything was chaotic. Brilliant light and thick smoke. The man with the machine gun opened fire, sensing that Alex must be somewhere near.

But Alex was already passing him and the bullets went wide, slicing into the first Bandit and killing the driver instantly. Somehow the second Bandit managed to get through, but then there was a thud, a scream and the sound of metal smashing into brick. The clatter of bullets stopped and Alex smiled grimly to himself, realizing what had happened. The man with the machine gun had just been run over by his friend on the bike.

His smile faded as yet another Smart car appeared from nowhere, still some distance away but already getting closer. How many of them were there? Surely Cray's people would decide they'd had enough and give it a rest. But then Alex remembered the flash drive in his pocket and knew that Cray would rip all Amsterdam apart to get it back.

There was a bridge ahead of him, an old-fashioned construction of wood and metal with thick cables and counterweights. It crossed a much wider canal and there was a single barge approaching it. Alex was puzzled. The bridge was far too low to allow the barge to pass. Then a red traffic light blinked on; the bridge began to lift.

Alex glanced back. The Smart car was about fifty metres behind him and this time there was nowhere to hide, nowhere else to go. He looked ahead of him. If he could just get to the other side of this canal, he really would be able to disappear. Nobody would be able to follow – at least not until the bridge had come down again. But it looked as if he was already too late. The bridge had split in half, both sections rising at the same speed, the gap over the water widening with every second.

The Smart car was accelerating.

Alex had no choice.

Feeling the pain, and knowing that he had reached the last reserves of his strength, Alex pushed down and the bike picked up speed. The car's engine was louder now, howling in his ears, but he didn't dare look back again. All his energy was focused on the rapidly rising bridge.

He hit the wooden surface when it was at a forty-five degree slant. Insanely he found himself think-ing of some long-forgotten maths lesson at school. A right-angled triangle. He could see it clearly on the board. And he was cycling up its side!

He wasn't going to make it. Every time he pushed down on the pedals it was a little harder, and he was barely halfway up the slope. He could see the gap – huge now – and the dark, cold water below. The car was right behind him. It was so close he could hear nothing apart from its engine, and the smell of petrol filled his nostrils.

He pedalled one last time – and at the same moment pressed the red button in the bell: the ejector seat. There was a soft explosion right below him. The saddle had rocketed off the bike, propelled by compressed air or some sort of ingenious hydraulic system. Alex shot into the air, over his side of the bridge, over the gap and then down onto the other side, rolling over and over as he tumbled all the way down. As he spun round, he saw the Smart car. Incredibly, it had tried to follow him. It was suspended in mid-air between the two halves of the bridge. He could see the driver's face, the open eyes, the gritted teeth. Then the car plunged down. There was a great splash and it sank at once beneath the black surface of the canal.

Alex got painfully to his feet. The saddle was lying next to him and he picked it up. There was a message underneath. He wouldn't have been able to read it while the saddle was attached to the frame. *If you can read this, you owe me a new bike*.

Smithers had a warped sense of humour. Carrying the saddle, Alex began to limp back to the hotel. He was too tired to smile.

EMERGENCY MEASURES

The Saskia Hotel was an old building that had somehow managed to elbow its way between a converted warehouse and a block of flats. There were just five bedrooms, stacked on top of each other like a house of cards, each one with a view of the canal. The flower market was a short walk away and even at night the air smelt sweet. Jack had chosen it because it was small and out of the way. Somewhere, she hoped, where they wouldn't be noticed.

When Alex opened his eyes at eight the following morning, he found himself lying on a bed in a small, irregularly shaped room on the top floor, built into the roof. He hadn't folded the shutters and sunlight was streaming in through the open window. Slowly he sat up, his body already complaining about the treatment it had received the night before. His clothes were neatly folded on a chair but he couldn't remember putting them there. He looked over to the side and saw a note taped to the mirror.

Breakfast served until ten.
Hope you can make it downstairs! xxx

He smiled, recognizing Jack's handwriting.

There was a tiny bathroom, hardly bigger than a cupboard, leading off the main room and Alex went in and washed. He cleaned his teeth, thankful for the taste of the peppermint. Even nearly ten hours later he hadn't quite forgotten the taste of the snake's blood. As he got dressed, he thought back to the night before when he had finally limped into the reception area to discover Jack waiting for him in one of the antique chairs. He hadn't thought he had been too badly hurt but the look on her face had told him differently. She had ordered sandwiches and hot chocolate from the puzzled receptionist, then led him to the tiny lift that carried them up five floors. Jack hadn't asked any questions and Alex had been grateful. He was too tired to explain, too tired to do anything.

Jack had made him take a shower, and by the time he had come out she had somehow managed to get her hands on a pile of plasters, bandages and antiseptic cream. Alex was sure he needed none of them and he was relieved when they were interrupted by the arrival of room service. He had thought he would be too tired to eat, but suddenly he found that he was ravenously hungry and wolfed down the lot while Jack watched. At last he had stretched out on the bed.

He was asleep the moment he closed his eyes.

Now he finished dressing, checked his bruises in the mirror, and went out. He took the creaking lift all the way down to a vaulted, low-ceilinged cellar underneath the reception area. This was where breakfast was served. It was a Dutch breakfast of cold meats, cheeses and bread rolls, served with coffee. Alex saw Jack sitting at a table on her own in a corner. He went over and joined her.

"Hi, Alex," she said. She was obviously relieved to see him looking more like his old self. "How did you sleep?"

"Like a log." He sat down. "Do you want me to tell you what happened last night?"

"Not yet. I have a feeling it'll put me off my breakfast."

They ate, and then he told her everything that had happened from the moment he had entered Cray's compound on the side of the truck. When he finished, there was a long silence. Jack's last cup of coffee had gone cold.

"Damian Cray is a maniac!" she exclaimed. "I'll tell you one thing, Alex, I'm never going to buy another of his CDs!" She sipped her coffee, grimaced and put the cup down. "But I still don't get it," she said. "What do you think he's doing, for heaven's sake? I mean ... Cray is a national hero. He sang at Princess Diana's wedding!"

"It was her birthday," Alex corrected her.

"And he's given zillions to charity. I went to one of his concerts once. Every penny he made went to Save the Children. Or maybe I got the name wrong; maybe it was Beat Up and Try to Kill the Children! Just what the hell is going on?"

"I don't know. The more I think about it, the less sense it makes."

"I don't even want to think about it. I'm just relieved you managed to get out of there alive. And I hate myself for letting you go in alone." She thought for a moment. "It seems to me you've done your bit," she went on. "Now you have to go back to MI6 and tell them what you know. You can take them the flash drive. This time they'll have to believe you."

"I couldn't agree with you more," Alex said. "But first of all we have to get out of Amsterdam. And we're going to have to be careful. Cray is bound to have people at the station. And at the airport for that matter."

Jack nodded. "We'll take a bus," she said. "We can go to Rotterdam or Antwerp. Maybe we can get a plane from there."

They had finished their breakfast. Now they packed, paid and left the hotel. Jack used cash. She was afraid that with all his resources, Cray might be able to track a credit card. They picked up a taxi at the flower market and took it out to the suburbs, where they caught a local bus. Alex realized it was going to be a long journey home, and that worried him. Twelve hours had passed since he had heard Cray announce that Eagle Strike would take place in two days' time. It was already the middle of the morning.

Less than thirty-six hours remained.

Damian Cray had woken early and was sitting up in a four-poster bed with mauve silk sheets and at least a dozen pillows. There was a tray in front of him, brought in by his personal maid along with the morning newspapers, specially flown over from England. He was eating his usual breakfast of organic porridge, Mexican honey (made by his own bees), soya milk and cranberries. It was well known that Cray was a vegetarian. At different times he had campaigned against battery farming, the transportation of live animals and the importation of goose liver pâté. This morning he had no appetite but he ate anyway. He had a personal dietitian who never let him forget it when he missed breakfast.

He was still eating when there was a knock at the door and Yassen Gregorovich came into the room.

"Well?" Cray demanded. It never bothered him having people in his bedroom. He had composed some of his best songs in bed.

"I've done what you said. I have men at Amsterdam Central, Amsterdam Zuid, Lelylaan, De Vlugtlaan ... all the local stations. There are also men at Schiphol Airport and I'm covering the ports. But I don't think Alex Rider will turn up at any of them."

"Then where is he?"

"If I were him, I'd head for Brussels or Paris. I have contacts in the police and I've got them looking out for him. If anybody sees him, we'll hear about it. But my guess is that we won't find him until he returns to England. He'll go straight to MI6 and the flash drive will go with him."

Cray threw down his spoon. "You seem very unconcerned about it all," he remarked.

Yassen said nothing.

"I have to say, I'm very disappointed in you, Mr Gregorovich. When I was setting up this operation, I was told you were the best. I was told you never made mistakes." There was still no answer. Cray scowled. "I was paying you a great deal of money. Well, you can forget that now. It's finished. It's all over. Eagle Strike isn't going to happen. And what about me? MI6 are bound to find out about all this and if they come after me..." His voice cracked. "This was meant to be my moment of glory. This was my life's work. Now it's been destroyed, and it's all thanks to you!"

"It's not finished," Yassen said. His voice hadn't changed, but there was an icy quality to it which might have warned Cray that once again he had come perilously close to a sudden and unexpected death. The Russian looked down at the little man, propped up on his pillows in the bed. "But we have to take emergency measures. I have people in England. I have given them instructions. You will have the flash drive returned to you in time."

"How are you going to manage that?" Cray asked. He didn't sound convinced.

"I have been considering the situation. All along I have believed that Alex has been acting on his own. That it was chance that brought him to us."

"He was staying at that house in the South of France."

"Yes."

"So how do you explain it?"

"Ask yourself this question. Why was Alex so upset by what happened to the journalist? It was none of his business. But he was angry. He risked his life coming onto the boat, the *Fer de Lance*. The answer is obvious. The friend he was staying with was a girl."

"A girlfriend?" Cray smiled sarcastically.

"He must obviously have feelings for her. That is what set him on our trail."

"And do you think this girl...?" Cray could see what the Russian was thinking, and suddenly the future didn't seem so bleak after all. He sank back into the pillows. The breakfast tray rose and fell in front of him.

"What's her name?" Cray asked.

"Sabina Pleasure," Yassen said.

* * *

Sabina had always hated hospitals and everything about the Whitchurch reminded her why.

It was huge. You could imagine walking through the revolving doors and never coming out again. You might die; you might simply be swallowed up by the system. It would make no difference. Everything about the building was impersonal, as if it had been specially designed to make the patients feel like factory products. Doctors and nurses were coming in and out, looking exhausted and defeated. Even being close to the place filled Sabina with a sense of dread.

The Whitchurch was a brand-new hospital in south London. Sabina's mother had brought her here. The two of them were in the car park, sitting together in Liz Pleasure's VW Golf.

"Are you sure you don't want me to come with you?" her mother was saying.

"No. I'll be all right."

"He is the same, Sabina. You have to know that. He's been hurt. You may be shocked by how he looks. But underneath it all he's still the same."

"Does he want to see me?"

"Of course he does. He's been looking forward to it. Just don't stay too long. He gets tired..."

It was the first time Sabina had visited her father since he had been airlifted back from

France. He hadn't been strong enough to see her until today and, she realized, the same was true of her. In a way, she had been dreading this. She had wondered what it would be like seeing him. He was badly burnt. He was still unable to walk. But in her dreams he was the same old dad. She had a photograph of him beside her bed and every night, before she went to sleep, she saw him as he had always been: shaggy and bookish but always healthy and smiling. She knew she would have to start facing reality the moment she walked into his room.

Sabina took a deep breath. She got out of the car and walked across the car park, past Accident and Emergency and into the hospital. The doors revolved and she found herself sucked into a reception area that was at once too busy and too brightly lit. Sabina couldn't believe how crowded and noisy it was – more like the inside of a shopping mall than a hospital. There were indeed a couple of shops, one selling flowers, and next to it a café and delicatessen where people could buy sandwiches and snacks to carry up to the friends and relatives they were visiting. Signs pointed in every direction. Cardiology. Paediatrics. Renal. Radiology. Even the names sounded somehow threatening.

Edward Pleasure was in Lister Ward, named after a nineteenth-century surgeon. Sabina knew that it was on the third floor but, looking around, she could see no sign of a lift. She was about to ask for directions when a man – a young doctor from the look of him – suddenly stepped into her path.

"Lost?" he asked. He was in his twenties, dark-haired, wearing a loose-fitting white coat and carrying a water cup. He looked as if he had stepped straight out of a television soap. He was smiling as if at some private joke and Sabina had to admit that maybe it was funny, her being lost when she was totally surrounded by signs.

"I'm looking for Lister Ward," Sabina said.

"That's on the third floor. I'm just going up there myself. But I'm afraid the lifts are out of order," the doctor added.

That was strange. Her mother hadn't mentioned it and she had been to the ward only the evening before. But Sabina imagined that in a hospital like this, things would break down all the time.

"There's a staircase you can take. Why don't you come along with me?"

The doctor crumpled his cup and dropped it in a bin. He walked through the reception area and Sabina followed.

"So who are you visiting?" the doctor asked.

"My dad."

"What's wrong with him?"

"He had an accident."

"That's too bad. How is he getting on?"

"This is the first time I've visited him. He's getting better ... I think."

They went through a set of double doors and down a corridor. Sabina noticed that they had left all the visitors behind them. The corridor was long and empty. It brought them to a hallway where five different passages converged. To one side was a staircase leading up, but the doctor ignored it. "Isn't that the way?" she asked.

"No." The doctor turned and smiled again. He seemed to smile a lot. "That goes up to Urology. You can get through to Lister Ward but this way's shorter." He gestured at a door and opened it. Sabina followed him through.

To her surprise she found herself back out in the open air. The door led into a partly covered area round the side of the hospital, where supply vehicles parked. There was a raised loading bay and a number of crates already stacked up. One wall was lined by a row of dustbins, each one a different colour according to what sort of refuse it was meant to take.

"Excuse me, I think you've—" Sabina began.

But then her eyes widened in shock. The doctor was lunging towards her, and before she knew what was happening he had grabbed her round the neck. Her first, and her only, thought was that he was some sort of madman, and her response was automatic. Sabina had been to self-defence classes; her parents had insisted. Without so much as hesitating, she whirled round, driving her knee between the man's legs. At the same time, she opened her mouth to scream. She had been taught that in a situation like this, noise was the one thing an attacker most feared.

But he was too fast for her. Even as the scream rose in her throat, his hand clamped tight over her mouth. He had seen what she was about to do and had twisted round behind her, one hand on her mouth, the other arm pinning her to him. Sabina knew now that she had assumed too much. The man had been wearing a white coat. He had been in the hospital. But of course he could have been anyone and she had been crazy to go with him. Never go anywhere with a stranger. How many times had her parents told her that?

An ambulance appeared, backing at speed into

the service area. Sabina felt a surge of hope that gave her new strength. Whatever her attacker was planning to do, he had chosen the wrong place. The ambulance had arrived just in time. But then she realized that the man hadn't reacted. She had thought he would let her go and run away. On the contrary, he had been expecting the ambulance and began dragging her towards it. Sabina stared as the back of the ambulance burst open and two more men jumped out. This whole thing had been planned! The three of them were in it together. They had known she would be there, visiting her father, and had come to the hospital meaning to intercept her.

Somehow she managed to bite the hand that was clamped over her mouth. The fake doctor swore and let go. Sabina lashed out with her elbow and felt it crash into the man's nose; he reeled backwards and suddenly she was free. She tried again to scream, to raise the alarm, but the two men from the ambulance were on her. One of them was holding something silver and pointed but Sabina only knew that it was a hypodermic syringe when she felt it jab into her arm. She squirmed and kicked, but she felt the strength rush out of her like water falling through a trapdoor. Her legs buckled and she would have fallen if the two men hadn't caught hold of her. She wasn't unconscious. Her thoughts were clear. She knew that she was in terrible danger – more danger than she had ever known – but she had no idea why this was happening.

Helplessly, Sabina was dragged towards the ambulance and thrown in. There was a mattress on the floor and at least that broke her fall. Then the doors slammed shut and she heard a lock being turned from the outside. She was trapped, on her own in an empty metal box, unable to move as the drug took effect. Sabina felt total despair.

The two men walked off into the hospital grounds as if nothing had taken place. The fake doctor removed his white coat and stuffed it into one of the bins. He was wearing an ordinary suit underneath and he saw that there was blood on the front of his shirt. His nose was bleeding, but that was good. When he went back into the hospital, he would simply look like one of the patients.

The ambulance drove slowly away. If anyone had bothered to look, they would have seen that the driver was dressed in exactly the same clothes as the other crews. Liz Pleasure actually noticed it leave, sitting in her VW in the car park. She was still there half an hour later, wondering what had happened to Sabina. But it would be a while yet before she realized that her daughter had disappeared.

UNFAIR EXCHANGE

It was five o'clock when Alex arrived at London's City Airport, the end of a long, frustrating day that had seen him travelling by road and by air across three countries. He and Jack had taken the bus from Amsterdam to Antwerp, arriving just too late for the lunchtime flight. They had killed three hours at the airport, finally boarding an old-fashioned Fokker 50 that seemed to take for ever crossing over to England. Alex wondered now if he had wasted too much time avoiding Damian Cray. A whole day had gone. But at least the airport was on the right side of London, not too far from Liverpool Street and the offices of MI6.

Alex intended to take the flash drive straight to Alan Blunt. He would have telephoned ahead but he couldn't be sure that Blunt would even take the call. One thing was certain. He wouldn't feel safe until he had handed over the device. Once MI6 had it in their hands, he would be able to relax.

That was his plan – but everything changed as he stepped into the arrivals hall. There was a woman sitting at a coffee bar reading the evening newspaper. The front page was open. It was almost as if it had been put there for Alex to see. A photograph of Sabina. And a headline:

SCHOOLGIRL DISAPPEARS
FROM HOSPITAL

"This way," Jack was saying. "We can get a cab."

"Jack!"

Jack saw the look on his face and followed his eyes to the newspaper. Without saying another word, she hurried into the airport's only shop and bought a copy for herself.

There wasn't very much to the story – but at this stage there wasn't a lot to tell. A fifteen-year-old schoolgirl from south London had been visiting her father at Whitchurch Hospital that morning. He had recently been injured in a terrorist incident in the South of France. Inexplicably she had never reached the ward, but instead had vanished into thin air. The police were urging any witnesses to come forward. Her mother had already made a television appeal for Sabina to come home.

"It's Cray," Alex said. His voice was empty. "He's got her."

"Oh God, Alex." Jack sounded as wretched as he felt. "He's done this to get the flash drive. We should have thought..."

"There was no way we could have expected this. How did he even know she was my friend?" Alex thought for a moment. "Yassen." He answered his own question. "He must have told Cray."

"You have to go to MI6 straight away. It's the only thing you can do."

"No. I want to go home first."

"Alex – why?"

Alex looked down at the picture one last time, then crumpled the page in his hands. "Cray may have left a message for me," he said.

There was a message. But it came in a form that Alex hadn't quite expected.

Jack had gone into the house first, checking to make sure there was no one waiting for them.

Then she called Alex. She looked grim as she stood at the front door.

"It's in the sitting room," she said.

"It" was a brand-new widescreen television. Someone had been into the house. They had brought the television and left it in the middle of the room. There was a webcam perched on top; a brand-new red cable snaked into a junction box in the wall.

"A present from Cray," Jack murmured.

"I don't think it's a present," Alex said.

There was a remote control next to the webcam. Reluctantly Alex picked it up. He knew he wasn't going to like what he was about to see, but there was no way he could ignore it. He turned the television on.

The screen flickered and cleared and suddenly he found himself face to face with Damian Cray. Somehow he wasn't surprised. He wondered if Cray had returned to England or if he was transmitting from Amsterdam. He knew that this was a live image and that his own picture would be sent back via the webcam. Slowly he sat down in front of the screen. He showed no emotion at all.

"Alex!" Cray looked relaxed and cheerful. His voice was so clear he could have been in the room with them. "I'm so glad you got back safely. I've been waiting to speak to you."

"Where's Sabina?" Alex asked.

"Where's Sabina? Where's Sabina? How very sweet! Young love!"

The image changed. Alex heard Jack gasp. Sabina was lying on a bunk in a bare room. Her hair was dishevelled but otherwise she seemed unhurt. She looked up at the camera and Alex could see the fear and confusion in her eyes.

Then the picture switched back to Cray. "We haven't damaged her ... yet," he said. "But that could change at any time."

"I'm not giving you the flash drive," Alex said.

"Hear me out, Alex." Cray leant forward so that he seemed to come closer to the screen. "Young people these days are so hot-headed! I've gone to a great deal of trouble and expense on account of you. And the thing is, you *are* going to give me the flash drive because if you don't your girl-friend is going to die, and you are going to see it on video."

"Don't listen to him, Alex!" Jack exclaimed.

"He *is* listening to me and I'd ask you not to interrupt!" Cray smiled. He seemed totally confident, as if this were nothing more than another celebrity interview. "I can imagine what's going through your mind," he went on, speaking again to Alex. "You're thinking of going to your friends at MI6. I would seriously advise against it."

"How do you know we haven't been to them already?" Jack asked.

"I very much hope you haven't," Cray replied. "Because I am a very nervous man. If I think anyone is making enquiries about me, I will kill the girl. If I find myself being watched by people I don't know, I will kill the girl. If a policeman so much as glances at me in the street, I may well kill the girl. And this I promise you. If you do not bring me the flash drive, personally, before ten o'clock tomorrow morning, I will certainly kill the girl."

"No!" Alex was defiant.

"You can lie to me, Alex, but you can't lie to yourself. You don't work for MI6. They mean nothing to you. But the girl does. If you abandon her, you'll regret it for the rest of your life. And it won't end with her. I will hunt down the rest of your friends. Don't underestimate my power! I will destroy everything and everyone you know. And then I will come after you. So don't kid yourself. Get it over with now. Give me what I want."

There was a long silence.

"Where can I find you?" Alex asked. The words tasted sour in his mouth. They tasted of defeat.

"I am at my house in Wiltshire. You can get a taxi from Bath station. All the drivers know where I live."

"If I bring it to you..." Alex found himself struggling to find the right words. "How do I know that you'll let her go? How do I know you'll let either of us go?"

"Exactly!" Jack had chipped in again. "How do we know we can trust you?"

"I'm a knight of the realm!" Cray exclaimed. "The Queen trusts me; you can too!"

The screen went blank.

Alex turned to Jack. For once he was helpless. "What do I do?" he asked.

"Ignore him, Alex. Go to MI6."

"I can't, Jack. You heard what he said. Before ten o'clock tomorrow morning. MI6 won't be able to do anything before then, and if they try something, Cray will kill Sab." He rested his head in his hands. "I couldn't allow that to happen. She's only in this mess because of me. I couldn't live with myself afterwards."

"But, Alex... A lot more people could get hurt if Eagle Strike – whatever it is – goes ahead."

"We don't know that."

"You think Cray would do all this if he was just going to rob a bank or something?"

Alex said nothing.

"Cray is a killer, Alex. I'm sorry. I wish I could be more helpful. But I don't think you can just walk into his house."

Alex thought about it. He thought for a long time. As long as Cray had Sabina, he held all the cards. But perhaps there was a way he could get her out of there. It would mean giving himself up. Once again he would become Cray's prisoner. But with Sabina free, Jack would be able to contact MI6. And perhaps – just perhaps – Alex might come out of this alive.

Quickly he outlined his idea to Jack. She listened – but the more she heard, the unhappier she looked.

"It's terribly dangerous, Alex," she said.

"But it might work."

"You can't give him the flash drive."

"I won't give him the flash drive, Jack."

"And if it all goes wrong?"

Alex shrugged. "Then Cray wins. Eagle Strike happens." He tried to smile, but there was no humour in his voice. "But at least we'll finally find out what it is."

*   *   *

The house was on the edge of the Bath valley, a twenty-minute drive from the station. Cray had been right about one thing. The taxi driver knew where it was without needing a map or an address – and as the car rolled down the private lane towards the main entrance, Alex understood why.

Damian Cray lived in an Italian convent. According to the newspapers, he had seen it in Umbria, fallen in love with it and shipped it over, brick by brick. The building really was extraordinary. It seemed to have taken over much of the surrounding countryside, cut off from public view by a tall, honey-coloured brick wall with two carved wooden gates at least ten metres high. Beyond the wall Alex could see a slanting roof of terracotta tiles, and beyond it an elaborate tower with pillars, arched windows and miniature battlements. Much of the garden had been imported from Italy too, with dark green, twisting cypresses and olive trees. Even the weather didn't seem quite English. The sun had come out and the sky was a radiant blue. It had to be the hottest day of the year.

Alex paid the driver and got out. He was wearing a pale grey, short-sleeved Trailrider cycling jersey without the elbow pads. As he walked down to the gates, he loosened the zip that ran up to the neck, allowing the breeze to play against his skin. There was a rope coming out of a hole in the wall and he pulled it. A bell rang out. Alex reflected that once this same bell might have called the nuns from their prayers. It seemed somehow wicked that a holy place should have been uprooted and brought here to be a madman's lair.

The gates opened electronically. Alex walked through and found himself in a cloister: a rectangle of perfectly mown grass surrounded by statues of saints. Ahead there was a fourteenth-century chapel with a villa attached, the two somehow existing in perfect harmony. He smelt lemons in the air. Pop music drifted from somewhere in the house. Alex recognized the song. *White Lines*: Cray was playing his own CD.

The front door of the house stood open. There was still nobody in sight, so Alex walked inside. The door led directly into a wide airy space with beautiful furniture arranged over a quarry-tiled floor. There was a grand piano made of rosewood, and a number of paintings, medieval altar pieces, were hanging on plain white walls. A row of six windows looked out onto a terrace with a garden beyond. White muslin curtains, hanging ceiling to floor, swayed gently in the breeze.

Damian Cray was sitting on an ornately carved wooden seat with a white poodle curled up in his lap. He glanced up as Alex came into the room. "Ah, there you are, Alex." He stroked the dog. "This is Bubbles. Isn't he beautiful?"

"Where's Sabina?" Alex asked.

Cray scowled. "I'm not going to be dictated to, if you don't mind," he said. "Especially not in my own home."

"Where is she?"

"All right!" The moment of anger had passed. Cray stood up and the dog jumped off his lap and ran out of the room. He crossed over to the desk and pressed a button. A few seconds later a door opened and Yassen Gregorovich came in. Sabina was with him. Her eyes widened when she saw Alex but she was unable to speak. Her hands were tied and there was a piece of tape across her mouth. Yassen forced her into a chair and stood over her. His eyes avoided Alex.

"You see, Alex, here she is," Cray said. "A little scared, perhaps, but otherwise unhurt."

"Why have you tied her up?" Alex demanded. "Why won't you let her talk?"

"Because she said some very hurtful things to me," Cray replied. "She also tried to assault me. In fact, frankly she has behaved in a very unladylike way." He scowled. "Now – you have something for me."

This was the moment that Alex had dreaded. He had a plan. Sitting on the train from London to Bath, in the taxi, and even walking into the house, he had been certain it would work. Now, facing Damian Cray, he suddenly wasn't so sure.

He reached into his pocket and took out the flash drive. The silver capsule had a lid, which Alex had opened, revealing a maze of circuitry inside. He had taped a brightly coloured tube in place, the nozzle pointing into the device. He held it up so that Cray could see.

"What is that?" Cray demanded.

"It's superglue," Alex replied. "I don't know what's inside your precious flash drive, but I doubt it'll work if it's gummed up with this stuff. I just have to squeeze my hand and you can forget Eagle Strike. You can forget the whole thing."

"How very ingenious!" Cray giggled. "But I don't actually see the point."

"It's simple," Alex said. "You let Sabina go; she walks out of here. She goes to a pub or a house and she telephones me here. You can give her the number. Once I know she's safe, I'll give you the flash drive."

Alex was lying.

As soon as Sabina had gone, he would squeeze the tube anyway. The flash drive would be filled with superglue, which would harden almost immediately. Alex was fairly sure it would make the device inoperable. He had no qualms about double-crossing Cray. It had been his plan all along. He didn't like to think what would happen to him, but that didn't matter. Sabina would be free. And as soon as Jack knew she was safe, she would be able to act. Jack would call MI6. Somehow Alex would have to stay alive until they arrived.

"Was this your idea?" Cray asked. Alex said nothing so he went on. "It's very clever. Very cute. But the question is..." He raised a finger on each hand. "Will it work?"

"I mean what I say." Alex held out the flash drive. "Let her go."

"But what if she goes straight to the police?"

"She won't."

Sabina tried to shout her disagreement from behind the gag. Alex took a breath.

"You'll still have me," he explained. "If Sabina goes to the police, you can do whatever you want to me. So that'll stop her. Anyway, she doesn't know what you're planning. There's nothing she can do."

Cray shook his head. "I'm sorry," he said.

"What?"

"No deal!"

"Are you serious?" Alex closed his hand around the tube.

"Entirely."

"What about Eagle Strike?"

"What about your girlfriend?" There was a heavy pair of kitchen scissors on the desk. Before Alex could say anything, Cray picked them up and threw them to Yassen. Sabina began to struggle furiously, but the Russian held her down. "You've made a simple miscalculation, Alex," Cray continued. "You're very brave. You would do almost anything to have the girl released. But I will do anything to keep her. And I wonder how much you'll be prepared to watch, how far I'll have to go, before you decide that you might as well give me the flash drive anyway. A finger, maybe? Two fingers?"

Yassen opened the scissors. Sabina had suddenly gone very quiet and still. Her eyes pleaded with Alex.

"No!" Alex yelled. With a wave of despair he knew that Cray had won. He had gambled on at least getting Sabina out of here. But it wasn't to be.

Cray saw the defeat in his eyes. "Give it to me!" he demanded.

"No."

"Start with the little finger, Yassen. Then we'll work one at a time towards her thumb."

Tears formed in Sabina's eyes. She couldn't hide her terror.

Alex felt sick. Sweat trickled down the sides of his body under his shirt. There was nothing more he could do. He wished now that he had listened to Jack. He wished he had never come.

He threw the flash drive onto the desk.

Cray picked it up.

"Well, that's got that sorted," he said with a smile. "Now, why don't we forget all this unpleasantness and go and have a cup of tea?"

INSANITY AND BISCUITS

Tea was served outside on the lawn – but it was a lawn the size of a field in a garden like nothing Alex had ever seen before. Cray had built himself a fantasy land in the English countryside, with dozens of pools, fountains, miniature temples and grottoes. There was a rose garden and a statue garden, a garden filled entirely with white flowers, and another given over to herbs, which had been laid out like sections in a clock. And all around him he had constructed replicas of buildings that Alex recognized. The Eiffel Tower, the Colosseum in Rome, the Taj Mahal, the Tower of London: each one was exactly one hundredth the scale of the original and all of them were jumbled together like picture postcards scattered on the floor. It was the garden of a man who wanted to rule the world but couldn't, and so had cut the world down to his own size.

"What do you think of it?" Cray asked as he joined Alex at the table.

"Some gardens have crazy paving," Alex replied quietly, "but I've never seen anything as crazy as this."

Cray smiled.

There were five of them sitting on the raised terrace outside the house: Cray, Alex, Yassen, the man called Henryk and Sabina. She had been untied and the gag taken off her mouth – and as soon as she had been freed, she had rushed over to Alex and thrown her arms around his neck.

"I'm so sorry," she had whispered. "I should have believed you."

That was all she had said. Apart from that she had been silent, her face pale. Alex knew that she was afraid. It was typical of Sabina not to want to show it.

"Well, here we all are. One happy family," Cray said. He pointed at the man with the silver hair and the pock-marked face. Now that he was closer to him, Alex could see that he was very ugly indeed. His eyes, magnified by the glasses, were slightly inflamed. He wore a denim shirt that was too tight and showed off his paunch.

"I don't think you've met Henryk," Cray added.

"I don't think I want to," Alex said.

"You mustn't be a bad loser, Alex. Henryk is very valuable to me. He flies jumbo jets."

Jumbo jets. Another piece of the puzzle.

"So where is he flying you?" Alex asked. "I hope it's somewhere far away."

Cray smiled to himself. "We'll come to that in a moment. In the meantime, shall I be mother? It's Earl Grey; I hope you don't mind. And do help yourself to a biscuit."

Cray poured five cups and set the pot down. Yassen hadn't spoken yet. Alex got the feeling that the Russian was uncomfortable being here. And that was another strange thing. He had always considered Yassen to be his worst enemy, but sitting here now he seemed almost irrelevant. This was all about Damian Cray.

"We have an hour before we have to leave," Cray said. "So I thought I might tell you a little about myself. I thought it might pass the time."

"I'm not really all that interested," Alex said.

Cray's smile grew a little thinner. "I can't believe that's true. You seem to have been interesting yourself in me for a considerable time."

"You tried to kill my father," Sabina said.

Cray turned round, surprised to hear her voice.

"Yes, that's right," he admitted. "And if you'll just shut up, I'm about to tell you why."

He paused. A pair of butterflies shimmered around a bed of lavender.

"I have had an extremely interesting and priv- ileged life," Cray began. "My parents were rich. Super rich, you might say. But not super. My father was a businessman and he was frankly rather boring. My mother didn't do anything very much; I didn't much like her either. I was an only child and naturally I was fabulously spoilt. I sometimes think that I was richer when I was eight years old than most people will be in their lifetime!"

"Do we have to listen to this?" Alex asked.

"If you interrupt me again, I'll ask Yassen to get the scissors," Cray replied. He went on. "I had my first serious row with my parents when I was thirteen. You see, they'd sent me to the Royal Academy in London. I was an extremely talented singer. But the trouble was, I hated it there. Bach and Beethoven and Mozart and Verdi. I was a teenager, for heaven's sake! I wanted to be Elvis Presley; I wanted to be in a pop group; I wanted to be famous!

"My father got very upset when I told him. He turned up his nose at anything popular. He really thought I'd failed him, and I'm afraid my mother agreed. They both had this idea that one day I'd be singing opera at Covent Garden or something ghastly like that. They didn't want me to leave. In fact, they wouldn't let me – and I don't know what would have happened if they hadn't had that extraordinary accident with the car. It fell on them, you know. I can't say I was terribly upset, although of course I had to pretend. But you know what I thought? I thought that God must be on my side. He wanted me to be a success and so He had decided to help me."

Alex glanced at Sabina to see how she was taking this. She was sitting rigidly in her chair, her cup of tea ignored. There was absolutely no colour in her face. But she was still in control. She wasn't giving anything away.

"Anyway," Cray continued, "the best thing was that my parents were out of the way and, even better, I had inherited all their money. When I was twenty-one, I bought myself a flat in London – actually it was more of a penthouse – and I set up my own band. We called ourselves Slam! As I'm sure you know, the rest is history. Five years later I went solo, and soon I was the greatest singer in the world. And that was when I started to think about the world I was in.

"I wanted to help people. All my life I've wanted to help people. The way you're looking at me, Alex, you'd think I'm some kind of monster. But I'm not. I've raised millions of pounds for charity. Millions and millions. And I should remind you, in case you've forgotten, that I have been knighted by the Queen. I am actually *Sir* Damian Cray, although I don't use the title because I'm no snob. A lovely lady, by the way, the Queen. Do you know how much money my Christmas single, 'Something for the Children', raised all on its own? Enough to feed a whole country!

"But the trouble is, sometimes being famous and being rich isn't enough. I *so* wanted to make a difference – but what was I to do when people wouldn't listen? I mean, take the case of the Milburn Institute in Bristol. This was a laboratory working for a number of cosmetics companies, and I discovered that they were testing many of their products on animals. Now, I'm sure you and I would be on the same side about this, Alex. I tried to stop them. I campaigned for over a year. We had a petition with twenty thousand signatures and still they wouldn't listen. So in the end – I'd met people and of course I had plenty of money – I suddenly realized that the best thing to do would be to have Professor Milburn killed. And that's what I did. And six months later the institute closed down and that was that. No more animals harmed."

Cray rotated a hand over the biscuit plate and picked one out. He was obviously pleased with himself.

"I had quite a lot of people killed in the years that followed," he said. "For example, there were some extremely unpleasant people cutting down the rainforest in Brazil. They're still in the rainforest ... six feet underneath it. Then there was a whole boatload of Japanese fishermen who wouldn't listen to me. I had them deep-frozen in their own freezer. That will teach them not to hunt rare whales! And there was a company in Yorkshire that was selling landmines. I didn't like them *at all*. So I arranged for the entire board of directors to disappear on an Outward Bound course in the Lake District and that put a stop to that!

"I've had to do some terrible things in my time. Really, I have." He turned to Sabina. "I did hate having to blow up your father. If he hadn't spied on me, it wouldn't have been necessary. But you must see that I couldn't let him spoil my plans."

Every cell in Sabina's body had gone rigid and

Alex knew she was having to force herself not to attack Cray. But Yassen was sitting right next to her and she wouldn't have got anywhere near.

Cray went on. "This is a terrible world, and if you want to make a difference, sometimes you have to be a bit extreme. And that's the point. I am extremely proud of the fact that I have helped so many people and so many different causes. Because helping people – *charity* – has been the work of my life."

He paused long enough to eat the biscuit he had chosen.

Alex forced himself to drink a little of the perfumed tea. He hated the taste but his mouth was completely dry. "I have a couple of questions," he said.

"Do, please, go ahead."

"My first one is for Yassen Gregorovich." He turned to the Russian. "Why are you working for this lunatic?" Alex wondered if Cray would hit him. But it would be worth it. All the signs indicated that the Russian didn't share Cray's world view. He seemed uncomfortable, out of place. It might be worth trying to sow a few seeds of discord between them.

Cray scowled, but did nothing. He signalled to Yassen to answer.

"He pays me," Yassen said simply.

"I hope your second question is more interesting," Cray snarled.

"Yes. You're trying to tell me that everything you've done is for a good cause. You think that all this killing is worth it because of the results. I'm not sure I agree. Lots of people work for charity; lots of people want to change the world. But they don't have to behave like you."

"I'm waiting..." Cray snapped.

"All right. This is my question. What is Eagle Strike? Are you really telling me it's a plan to make the world a better place?"

Cray laughed softly. For a moment he looked like the diabolical schoolboy he had once been, welcoming his own parents' death. "Yes," he said. "That's exactly what it is. Sometimes great people are misunderstood. You don't understand me and neither does your girlfriend. But I really do want to change the world. That's all I've ever wanted. And I've been very fortunate because my music has made it possible. In the twenty-first century, entertainers are much more influential than politicians or statesmen. I'm the only one who's actually noticed it."

Cray chose a second biscuit – a custard cream.

"Let me ask you a question, Alex. What do you

think is the greatest evil on this planet today?"

"Is that including or not including you?" Alex asked.

Cray frowned. "Please don't irritate me," he warned.

"I don't know," Alex said. "You tell me."

"Drugs!" Cray spat out the single word as if it were obvious. "Drugs are causing more unhappiness and destruction than anything anywhere in the world. Drugs kill more people than war or terrorism. Did you know that drugs are the single biggest cause of crime in western society? We've got kids out on the street taking heroin and cocaine, and they're stealing to support their habits. But they're not criminals; they're victims. It's the drugs that are to blame."

"We've talked about this at school," Alex said. The last thing he needed right now was a lecture.

"All my life I've been fighting drugs," Cray went on. "I've done advertisements for the government. I've spent millions building treatment centres. And I've written songs. You must have listened to *White Lines*..."

He closed his eyes and hummed softly, then sang:

"The poison's there. The poison flows
It's everywhere – in heaven's name

Why is it that no one knows
How to end this deadly game?"
He stopped.

"But I know how to end it," he said simply. "I've worked it out. And that's what Eagle Strike is all about. A world without drugs. Isn't that something to dream about, Alex? Isn't that worth a few sacrifices? Think about it! The end of the drug problem. And I can make it happen."

"How?" Alex was almost afraid of the answer.

"It's easy. Governments won't do anything. The police won't do anything. No one can stop the dealers. So you have to go back to the supplies. You have to think where these drugs come from. And where is that? I'll tell you...

"Every year, hundreds and hundreds of tons of heroin come from Afghanistan – in particular the provinces of Nangarhar and Helmand. Did you know production has increased by fourteen hundred per cent since the Taliban were defeated? So much for that particular war! Then, after Afghanistan, there's Burma and the golden triangle, with about one hundred thousand hectares of land used to produce opium and heroin. The government of Burma doesn't care. Nobody cares. And let's not forget Pakistan, manufacturing one hundred and fifty-five metric tons of opium a year, with refineries throughout the Khyber region and along the borders.

"On the other side of the world there's Colombia. It's the leading supplier and distributor of cocaine, but it also supplies heroin and marijuana. It's a business worth three billion dollars a year, Alex. Eighty tons of cocaine every twelve months. Seven tons of heroin. A lot of it ends up on the streets of American cities. In high schools. A tidal wave of misery and crime.

"But that's only a small part of the picture." Cray held up a hand and began to tick off other countries on his fingers. "There are refineries in Albania. Mule trains in Thailand. Coca crops in Peru. Opium plantations in Egypt. Ephedrine, the chemical used in heroin production, is manufactured in China. One of the biggest drugs markets in the world can be found in Tashkent, in Uzbekistan.

"These are the principal sources of the world's drug problem. This is where the trouble all starts. These are my targets."

"Targets..." Alex whispered the single word.

Damian Cray reached into his pocket and took out the flash drive. Yassen was suddenly alert. Alex knew he had a gun and would use it if he so much as moved.

"Although you weren't to know it," Cray explained, "this is actually a key to unlock one of the most complicated security systems ever devised. The original key was created by the National Security Agency and it is carried by the president of the United States. My friend, the late Charlie Roper, was a senior officer with the NSA, and it was his expertise, his knowledge of the codes, that allowed me to manufacture a duplicate. Even so, it has taken enormous effort. You have no idea how much computer processing power was required to create a second key."

"The Gameslayer..." Alex said.

"Yes. It was the perfect cover. So many people; so much technology. A plant with all the processing power I could ask for. And in reality it was all for this!"

He held up the little metal capsule.

"This key will give me access to two and a half thousand nuclear missiles. These are American missiles and they are on hair-trigger alert – meaning that they can be launched at a moment's notice. It is my intention to override the NSA's system and to fire twenty-five of those missiles at targets I have carefully chosen around the globe."

Cray smiled sadly.

"It is almost impossible to imagine the devastation that will be caused by twenty-five one-hundred-ton missiles exploding at the same time. South America, Central America, Asia, Africa ... almost every continent will feel the pain. And there will be pain, Alex. I am well aware of that.

"But I will have wiped out the poppy fields. The farms and the factories. The refineries, the trade routes, the markets. There will be no more drug suppliers because there will be no more drug supplies. Of course, millions will die. But millions more will be saved.

"That is what Eagle Strike is all about, Alex. The start of a new golden age. A day when all humanity will come together and rejoice.

"That day is now. My time has finally arrived."

EAGLE STRIKE

Alex and Sabina were taken to a room somewhere in the basement of the house and thrown inside. The door closed and suddenly they were alone.

Alex signalled to Sabina not to speak, then began a quick search. The door was a slab of solid oak, locked from the outside and probably bolted too. There was a single square window set high up in the wall, but it was barred and wouldn't have been big enough to crawl through anyway. There was no view. The room might once have been used to store wine; the walls were bare and undecorated, the floor concrete, and apart from a few shelves there was no furniture. A naked bulb hung on a wire from the ceiling. Alex was looking for hidden bugs. It was unlikely that Cray would want to eavesdrop on the two of them, but even so he wanted to be sure that they couldn't be overheard.

It was only when Alex had gone over every inch of the room that he turned to Sabina. She seemed amazingly calm. He thought about all the things that had happened to her. She had been kidnapped and kept prisoner – bound and gagged. She had been brought face to face with the man who had ordered the execution of her father, and had listened as he outlined his mad idea to destroy half the world. And here she was locked up again with the near certainty that she and Alex wouldn't be allowed to leave here alive. Sabina should have been terrified. But she simply waited quietly while Alex completed his checks, watching him as if seeing him for the first time.

"Are you OK?" he asked at last.

"Alex..." It was only when she tried to speak that the emotion came. She took a breath and fought for control. "I don't believe this is happening," she said.

"I know. I wish it wasn't." Alex didn't know what to say. "When did they get you?" he asked.

"At the hospital. There were three of them."

"Did they hurt you?"

"They scared me. And they gave me some sort

of injection." She scowled. "God – Damian Cray is such a creep! And I never realized he was so – *small*!"

That made Alex smile despite everything. Sabina hadn't changed.

But she was serious. "As soon as I saw him, I thought of you. I knew you'd been telling the truth all along and I felt so rotten for not believing you." She stopped. "You really are what you said. A spy!"

"Not exactly..."

"Do MI6 know you're here?"

"No."

"But you must have some sort of gadgets. You told me they gave you gadgets. Haven't you got exploding shoelaces or something to get us out of here?"

"I haven't got anything. MI6 don't even know I'm here. After what happened at the bank – in Liverpool Street – I sort of went after Cray on my own. I was just so angry about the way they tricked you and lied about me. I was stupid. I mean, I had the flash drive in my hand ... and I gave it back to Cray!"

Sabina understood. "You came here to rescue me," she said.

"Some rescue!"

"After the way I treated you, you should have just dumped me."

"I don't know, Sab. I thought I had it all worked out. I thought they'd let you go and everything would turn out all right. I had no idea..." Alex kicked out at the door. It was as solid as a rock. "We have to stop him," he said. "We have to do something."

"Maybe he was making it up," Sabina suggested. "Think about it. He said he was going to fire twenty-five missiles all around the world. American missiles. But they're all controlled from the White House. Only the American president can set them off. Everyone knows that. So what's he going to do? Fly to Washington and try to break in?"

"I wish you were right." Alex shook his head. "But Cray's got a huge organization. He's put years of planning and millions of pounds into this. He's got Yassen Gregorovich working for him. He must know something we don't."

He went over to her. He wanted to put an arm round her but he ended up standing awkwardly in front of her instead. "Listen," he said. "This is going to sound really big-headed and you know I'd never normally tell you what to do. But the thing is, I have sort of been here before..."

"What? Locked up by a maniac who wants to destroy the world?"

"Well, yes. Actually I have." He sighed. "My uncle was trying to turn me into a spy when I was still in short trousers. I never even realized it. And it's true what I told you. They made me train with the SAS. Anyway, the truth is ... I know things. And it may be that we do get a chance to get back at Cray. But if that happens, you have to leave everything to me. You have to do what I say. Without arguing..."

"Forget it!" Sabina shook her head. "I'll do what you say. But it was my dad he tried to kill. And I can tell you, if Cray leaves a kitchen knife lying around, I'm going to shove it somewhere painful..."

"It may already be too late," Alex said gloomily. "Cray may just leave us here. He could have already left."

"I don't think so. I think he needs you; I don't know why. Maybe it's because you came closest to beating him."

"I'm glad you're here," Alex said.

Sabina looked at him. "I'm not."

Ten minutes later the door opened and Yassen Gregorovich appeared carrying two sets of what looked like white overalls with red markings

– serial numbers – on the sleeves. "You are to put these on," he said.

"Why?" Alex asked.

"Cray wants you. You're coming with us. Do as you're told."

But Alex still hesitated. "What is this?" he demanded. There was something disturbingly familiar about what he was being asked to wear.

"It is a polyamide fabric," Yassen explained. The words meant nothing to Alex. "It is used in biochemical warfare," he added. "Now put it on."

With a growing sense of dread, Alex put the suit on over his own clothes. Sabina did the same. The overalls covered them completely, with hoods that would go over their heads. Alex realized that when they were fully suited up, they would be virtually shapeless. It would be impossible to tell that they were teenagers.

"Now come with me," Yassen said.

They were led back through the house and out into the cloister. There were now three vehicles parked on the grass: a jeep and two covered trucks, both painted white with the same red markings as the suits. There were about twenty men, all in biochemical suits. Henryk, the Dutch pilot, was in the back of the jeep, nervously polishing his glasses. Damian Cray stood next to him talking, but seeing Alex he stopped and came over. He was bristling with excitement, walking jauntily, his eyes even brighter than normal.

"So you're here!" he exclaimed, as if welcoming Alex to a party. "Excellent! I've decided I want you to come along. Mr Gregorovich tried to talk me out of it, but that's the thing about Russians. No sense of humour. But you see, Alex, none of this would have happened without you. You brought me the flash drive; it's only fair you should see how I use it."

"I'd rather see you arrested and sent to Broadmoor," Alex said.

Cray simply laughed. "That's what I like about you!" he exclaimed. "You're so rude. But I do have to warn you, Yassen will be watching you like a hawk. Or maybe I should say like an eagle. If you do anything at all, if you so much as blink without permission, he'll shoot your girlfriend first. And then he'll shoot you. Do you understand?"

"Where are we going?" Alex asked.

"We're taking the motorway into London. It'll take us just a couple of hours. You and Sabina will be in the first truck with Yassen. Eagle Strike has begun, by the way. Everything is in place. I think you'll enjoy it."

He turned his back on them and went over

to the jeep. A few minutes later the convoy left, rolling out of the gates and back up the lane to the main road. Alex and Sabina sat next to each other on a narrow wooden bench. There were six men with them, all armed with automatic rifles, slung over the white suits. Alex thought he recognized one of the faces from the compound outside Amsterdam. Certainly he knew the type. Pale skin, dead-looking hair, dark, empty eyes. Yassen sat opposite them. He too had put on a biochemical suit. He seemed to be staring at Alex, but he said nothing and his face was unreadable.

They travelled for two hours, taking the M4 towards London. Alex glanced occasionally at Sabina and she caught his eye once and smiled nervously. This wasn't her world. The men, the machine guns, the biochemical suits ... they were all part of a nightmare that had come out of nowhere and which still made no sense – with no sign of a way out. Alex was baffled too. But the suits suggested a dreadful possibility. Did Cray have biochemical weapons? Was he planning to use them?

At last they turned off the motorway. Looking out of the back flap, Alex saw a signpost to Heathrow Airport and suddenly he knew, without being told, that this was their true destination. He remembered the plane he had seen at the compound. And Cray, talking to him in the garden. *Henryk is very valuable to me. He flies jumbo jets.* The airport had to be part of it, but it still didn't explain so many things. The president of the United States. Nuclear missiles. The very name – Eagle Strike – itself. Alex was angry with himself. It was all there in front of him. Some sort of picture was taking shape. But it was still blurred, out of focus.

They stopped. Nobody moved. Then Yassen spoke for the first time. "Out!" A single word.

Alex went first, then helped Sabina down. He enjoyed feeling her hand in his. There was a sudden loud roar overhead and he looked up just in time to see an aircraft sweeping down out of the sky. He saw where they were. They had stopped on the top floor of an abandoned multi-storey car park – a legacy of Sir Arthur Lunt, Cray's father. It was on the very edge of Heathrow Airport, near the main runway. The only car, apart from their own, was a burnt-out shell. The ground was strewn with rubble and old rusting oil drums. Alex couldn't imagine why they had come here. Cray was waiting for a signal. Something was going to happen. But what?

Alex looked at his watch. It was exactly half past two. Cray called them over. He had travelled in the jeep with Henryk and now Alex saw that there was a radio transmitter on the back seat. Henryk turned a dial; there was a loud whine. Cray was certainly making a performance out of this. The radio had been connected to a loudspeaker so that they could all hear.

"It's about to begin," Cray said. He giggled. "Exactly on time!"

Alex looked up. A second plane was coming in. It was still too far away and too high up to be seen clearly, but even so, he thought he recognized something about its shape. Suddenly a voice crackled out of the loudspeaker in the jeep.

"Attention, air traffic control. This is Millennium Air flight 118 from Amsterdam. We have a problem."

The voice had been speaking in English but with a heavy Dutch accent. There was a pause, an empty hissing, and then a woman's voice replied. "Roger, MA 118. What is your problem, over?"

"Mayday! Mayday!" The voice from the aircraft was suddenly louder. "This is flight MA 118. We have a fire on board. Request immediate clearance to land."

Another pause. Alex could imagine the panic

in the control tower at Heathrow. But when the woman spoke again, her voice was professional, calm. "Roger your mayday. We have you on radar. Steer on 0-90. Descend three thousand feet."

"Air traffic control." The radio crackled again. "This is Captain Schroeder from flight MA 118. I have to advise you that I am carrying extremely hazardous biochemical products on behalf of the Ministry of Defence. We have an emergency situation here. Please advise."

The Heathrow woman replied immediately. "We need to know what is on board. Where is it and what are the quantities?"

"Air traffic control, we are carrying a nerve gas. We cannot be more specific. It is highly experimental and extremely dangerous. There are three canisters in the hold. We now have a fire in the main cabin. Mayday! Mayday!"

Alex looked again. The plane was much lower now and he knew exactly where he had seen it before. It was the cargo plane that he had seen in the compound outside Amsterdam. Smoke was streaming out of the side and even as Alex watched, flames suddenly exploded, spreading over the wings. To anyone watching, it would seem that the plane was in terrible danger. But Alex knew that the whole thing had been faked.

The control tower was monitoring the plane. "Flight MA 118, the emergency services have been alerted. We are beginning an immediate evacuation of the airport. Please proceed to twenty-seven left. You are cleared to land."

At once Alex heard the sound of alarms coming from all over the airport. The plane was still two or three thousand feet up, the flames trailing behind it. He had to admit that it looked totally convincing. Suddenly everything was starting to make sense. He was beginning to understand Cray's plan.

"Time to roll!" Cray announced.

Alex and Sabina were led back to the truck. Cray climbed into the jeep next to Henryk, who was driving, and they set off. It was difficult for Alex to see what was happening now as he only had a view out of the back, but he guessed that they had left the car park and were following the perimeter fence around the airport. The alarms seemed to have got louder; presumably they were getting nearer to them. A number of police sirens erupted in the distance and Alex noticed that the road had got busier as cars tore past, the drivers desperate to get away from the immediate area.

"What's he doing?" Sabina whispered.

"The plane isn't on fire," Alex said. "Cray's

tricked them. He's evacuating the airport. That's how we're going to get in."

"But why?"

"Enough," Yassen said. "You don't speak now." He reached under his seat and produced two gas masks which he handed to Alex and Sabina. "Put these on."

"Why do I need it?" Sabina asked.

"Just do as I say."

"Well, it'll ruin my make-up." She put it on anyway.

Alex did the same. All the men in the truck, including Yassen, had gas masks. Suddenly they were completely anonymous. Alex had to admit that there was a certain genius to Cray's scheme. It was a perfect way to break into the airport. By now all the security personnel would know that a plane carrying a deadly nerve agent was about to crash-land. The airport was in the throes of a full-scale emergency evacuation. When Cray and his miniature army arrived at the main gate, it was unlikely that anyone would ask them for ID. In their biochemical suits they looked official. They were driving official-looking vehicles. The fact that they had arrived at the airport in record time wouldn't be seen as suspicious. It was more like a miracle.

It happened exactly as Alex suspected.

The jeep stopped at a gate on the south side of the airport. The guards there were both young. One of them had only been in the job for a couple of weeks and was already panicking, faced with a red alert. The cargo plane hadn't landed yet but it was getting closer and closer, stumbling out of the air. The fire was worse, clearly out of control. And here were two trucks and an army vehicle filled with men in white suits, hoods and gas masks. He wasn't going to argue.

Cray leant out of the door. He was as anonymous as the rest of his men, his face concealed behind the gas mask. "Ministry of Defence," he snapped. "Biochemical Weapons division."

"Go ahead!" The guards couldn't hurry them through fast enough.

The plane touched down. Two fire engines and an assortment of emergency vehicles began to race towards it. Their truck overtook the jeep and came to a halt. Looking out of the back, Alex saw everything.

It started with Damian Cray.

He was sitting in the passenger seat of the jeep and had produced a radio transmitter. "It's time to raise the stakes," he said. "Let's make this a real emergency."

Somehow Alex knew what was about to happen. Cray pressed a button and at once the plane exploded, disappearing in a huge fireball that erupted out of it and at the same time consumed it. Fragments of wood and metal spun in all directions. Burning aviation fuel spilt over the runway, seeming to set it alight too. The emergency vehicles had fanned out as if to surround the wreckage, but then Alex realized that they had received new orders from the control tower. There was nothing more they could do. The pilot and his crew on the plane were certainly dead. Some unknown nerve gas could even now be leaking into the atmosphere. Turn round. Get out of there. Go!

Alex knew that Cray had cheated whoever had flown the plane, killing them with exactly the same cold-blooded ruthlessness with which he killed anyone who got in his way. The pilot would have been paid to send out the false alarm and then to fake a crash landing. He wouldn't have known that there was a load of plastic explosive concealed on board. He might have expected a long stay in an English prison. He hadn't been told his job was to die.

Sabina wasn't watching. Alex couldn't see anything of her face – the gas mask had fogged up –

but her head was turned away. For a moment he felt desperately sorry for her. What had she got into? And to think that this had all begun with a holiday in the South of France!

The truck jerked forward. They were inside the airport. Cray had managed to short-circuit the entire security system. Nobody would notice them – at least not for a while. But the questions still remained. What had they come for? Why here?

And then they slowed down one last time. Alex looked out. And at last everything made sense.

They had stopped in front of a plane, a Boeing 747-200B. But it was much more than that. Its body had been painted blue and white, with the words UNITED STATES OF AMERICA written across the main fuselage and the Stars and Stripes emblazoned on its tail. And there was the eagle, clutching a shield, just below the door, mocking Alex for not having guessed before. The eagle that had given Eagle Strike its name. It was the presidential seal and this was the presidential plane, Air Force One. This was the reason why Damian Cray was here.

Alex had seen it on the television in Blunt's office. The plane that had brought the American president to England. It flew him all over the world, travelling at just below the speed of sound. Alex knew very little about it, but then virtually all information about Air Force One was restricted. But one thing he did know. Just about anything that could be done in the White House could be done on the plane, even while it was in the air.

Just about anything. Including starting a nuclear war.

There were two men standing guard on the steps that led up to the open door and the main cabin. They were soldiers, dressed in khaki combat gear and black berets. As Cray got out of the car, they brought up their guns, moving into a position of alert. They had heard the alarms. They knew something was happening at the airport but they weren't sure what it had to do with them.

"What's going on?" one of them asked.

Damian Cray said nothing. His hand came up and suddenly he was holding a pistol. He fired twice, the bullets making hardly any sound – or perhaps the noise of the gun was somehow dwarfed by the immensity of the plane. The soldiers twisted round and fell onto the tarmac. Nobody had seen what had happened. All eyes were on the runway and the still-burning debris of the cargo plane.

Alex felt a surge of hatred for Cray, for his cowardice. The American soldiers hadn't been expecting trouble. The president was nowhere near the airport. Air Force One wasn't due to take off for another day. Cray could have knocked them out; he could have taken them prisoner. But it had been easier to kill them; already he was putting the gun back into his pocket, two human lives simply brushed aside and forgotten. Sabina stood next to him, staring in disbelief.

"Wait here," Cray said. He had removed his gas mask. His face was flushed with excitement.

Yassen Gregorovich and half the men ran up the steps onto the plane. The other half stripped off their white suits to reveal American army uniforms underneath. Cray hadn't missed a trick. If anyone did chance to turn their attention away from the cargo plane, it would seem that Air Force One was under heavy guard and that everything was normal. In fact, nothing could have been further from the truth.

More gunfire came from inside the plane. Cray was taking no prisoners. Anyone in his way was being finished without hesitation, without mercy.

Cray stood next to Alex. "Welcome to the VIP lounge," he said. "You might like to know, that's what they call this whole section of the airport."

He pointed at a glass and steel building on the other side of the plane. "That's where they all go. Presidents, prime ministers ... I've been in there once or twice as a matter of fact. Very comfortable, and no queues for passport control!"

"Let us go," Alex said. "You don't need us."

"Would you rather I killed you now, instead of later?"

Sabina glanced at Alex but said nothing.

Yassen appeared at the door of the plane and signalled. Air Force One had been taken. There was no one left to fight. Cray's men filed past him and made their way back down the stairs. One of them had been wounded; there was blood on the sleeve of his suit. So at least someone had tried to fight back!

"I think we can go on board," Cray said.

All his men were now dressed as American soldiers, forming a half circle round the steps leading up to the door of the plane, a defensive wall in the event of a counter-attack. Henryk had already climbed up; Alex and Sabina followed him. Cray was right behind them, holding his gun. So there were only going to be the five of them on the plane. Alex filed the information somewhere in his mind. At least the odds had been shortened.

Sabina was numb, walking as if hypnotized. Alex knew what she was feeling. His own legs almost refused to carry him, to take these steps, reserved for the most powerful man on the planet. As the door loomed up ahead, with another eagle mounted on its side, he saw Yassen appear from inside, dragging a body dressed in blue trousers and a blue waistcoat: one of the air stewards. Another innocent man sacrificed for Cray's mad dream.

Alex entered the plane.

Air Force One was like no other plane in the world. There were no seats cramped together, no economy class, nothing that looked even remotely like the inside of an ordinary jumbo jet. It had been modified for the president and his staff over three floors: offices and bedrooms, a conference room and kitchen ... four thousand square feet of cabin space in all. Somewhere inside, there was even an operating table, although it had never been used. Alex found himself in an open-plan living area. Everything had been designed for comfort, with a thick-pile carpet, low sofas and armchairs, and tables with old-fashioned electric lamps. The predominant colours were beige and brown, softly lit by dozens of lights recessed into the ceiling. A long corridor led down one side of the plane, with a series of smart offices and seating areas branching off. There were more sofas and occasional tables at intervals all the way down. The windows were covered with fawn-coloured blinds.

Yassen had cleared away the bodies but he had left a bloodstain on the carpet. It was horribly noticeable. The rest of the plane had been cleaned and vacuumed until it was spotless. There was a wheeled trolley against one of the walls and Alex noticed the gleaming crystal glasses, each one engraved with the words AIR FORCE ONE and a picture of the plane. A number of bottles stood on the lower shelf of the trolley: rare malt whiskies and vintage wines. It was service with a smile, all right. To fly on this plane was a privilege enjoyed by only a handful of people and they would be surrounded by total luxury.

Even Cray, who had his own private jet, looked impressed. He glanced at Yassen. "Is that it?" he asked. "Have we killed everyone who needs killing?"

Yassen nodded.

"Then let's get started. I'll take Alex. I want to show him... You wait here."

Cray nodded at Alex. Alex knew he had no

choice. He took one last glance at Sabina and tried to tell her with his eyes: *I'll think of something. I'll get us out of here.* But somehow he doubted it. The enormity of Eagle Strike had finally hit him. Air Force One! The presidential plane. It had never been invaded in this way – and no wonder. Nobody else would have been mad enough to consider it.

Cray jabbed Alex with the gun, forcing him up a stairway. Half of him hoped they would meet someone. Just one soldier or one member of the cabin crew who had managed to escape and who might be lying in wait. But he knew that Yassen would have been thorough in his work. He had told Cray that the entire crew had been dealt with. Alex didn't like to think how many men and women there might have been on board.

They entered a room filled with electronic equipment from floor to ceiling. Hugely sophisticated computers stood next to elaborate telephone and radar systems with banks of buttons, switches and blinking lights. Even the ceiling was covered with machinery. Alex realized he was standing in the communications centre of Air Force One. Someone must have been working there when Cray took over the plane. The door wasn't locked.

"Nobody at home," Cray said. "I'm afraid they weren't expecting visitors. We have the place to ourselves." He took the flash drive out of his pocket. "This is the moment of truth, Alex," he said. "This is all thanks to you. But do, please, stay very still. I don't want to kill you until you've seen this, but if you so much as blink, I'm afraid I may have to shoot you."

Cray knew what he was doing. He laid the gun on the table next to him so that it would never be more than a few centimetres from his hand. Then he opened the flash drive and plugged it into a socket in the front of the computer. Finally he sat down and tapped out a series of commands on the keyboard.

"I can't explain exactly how this works," he said as he continued. "We don't have time, and anyway I've always found computers and all that stuff really dreary. But these computers here are just like the ones in the White House, and they're connected to Mount Cheyenne, which is where our American friends have their top-secret underground nuclear weapons control centre. Now, the first things you need to set off the nuclear missiles are the launch codes. They change every day and they're sent to the president, wherever he is, by the National Security Agency. I hope

I am not boring you, Alex?"

Alex didn't reply. He was looking at the gun, measuring distances...

"The president carries them with him all the time. Did you know that President Carter actually lost the codes once? He sent them to the dry-cleaner's. But that's another story. The codes are transmitted by Milstar – the Military Strategic and Tactical Relay system. It's a satellite communications system. One set goes to the Pentagon and one set comes here. The codes are inside the computer and..."

There was a buzzing sound and a number of lights on the control panel suddenly went green. Cray let out a cry of pleasure. His face glowed green in the reflection.

"...and here they are now. Wasn't that quick! Strange though it may seem, I am now in control of just about all the nuclear missiles in the United States. Isn't that fun?"

He tapped more quickly on the keyboard and for a moment he was transformed. As his fingers danced over the keys, Alex was reminded of the Damian Cray he had seen playing the piano at Earls Court and Wembley Stadium. There was a dreamy smile on his face and his eyes were far away.

"There is, of course, a fail-safe device built into it all," he continued. "The Americans wouldn't want just anyone firing off their missiles, would they! No. Only the president can do it, because of this..."

Cray took a small silver key out of his pocket. Alex guessed that it must be a duplicate, also provided by Charlie Roper. Cray inserted it into a complicated-looking silver lock built into the workstation and opened it. There were two red buttons underneath. One to launch the missiles. The other marked with two words which were of more interest to Alex. SELF-DESTRUCT.

Cray was only interested in the first of them.

"This is the button," he said. "The big button. The one you've read all about. The button that means the end of the world. But it's fingerprint sensitive. If it isn't the president's finger, then you might as well go home." He reached out and pressed the launch button. Nothing happened. "You see? It doesn't work!"

"Then all this has been a waste of time!" Alex said.

"Oh no, my dear Alex. Because, you see, you may remember that I recently had the privilege – the very great privilege – of shaking hands with the president. I insisted on it. It was that important to me. But I had a special latex coating on my own hand, and when we shook, I took a cast of his fingers. Isn't that clever?"

Cray removed what looked like a thin plastic glove from his pocket and slipped it onto his hand. Alex saw that the fingers of the glove were moulded. He understood. The president's fingerprints had been duplicated onto the latex surface.

Cray now had the power to launch his nuclear attack.

"Wait a minute," Alex said.

"Yes?"

"You're wrong. You're terribly wrong. You think you're making things better, but you're not!" He struggled to find the right words. "You'll kill thousands of people. Hundreds of thousands of people, and most of them will be innocent. They won't have anything to do with drugs..."

"There have to be sacrifices. But if a thousand people die to save a million, what's so wrong with that?"

"Everything is wrong with it! What about the fallout? Have you thought what it'll do to the rest of the planet? I thought you cared about the environment. But you're going to destroy it."

"It's a price worth paying, and one day the

whole world will agree. You've got to be cruel to be kind."

"You only think that because you're insane."

Cray reached for the launch button.

Alex dived forward. He no longer cared about his own safety. He couldn't even protect Sabina. The two of them might be killed, but he had to stop this happening. He had to protect the millions who would die all over the world if Cray was allowed to continue. Twenty-five nuclear missiles falling simultaneously out of the sky! It was beyond imagination.

But Cray had been expecting the move. Suddenly the gun was in his hand and his arm was swinging through the air. Alex felt a savage blow on the side of his head as Cray struck him. He was thrown back, dazed. The room swam in front of his eyes, and he stumbled and fell.

"Too late," Cray muttered.

He reached out and drew a circle in the air with a single finger.

He paused.

Then he stabbed down.

"FASTEN YOUR SEAT BELTS"

The missiles had been activated.

All over America, in deserts and in mountains, on roads and railways, even out at sea, the launch sequences began automatically. Bases in North Dakota, Montana and Wyoming suddenly went onto red alert. Sirens howled. Computers went into frantic overdrive. It was the start of a panic that would spread in minutes all around the world.

And one by one the twenty-five rockets blasted into the air in a moment of terrible beauty.

Eight Minutemen, eight Peacekeepers, five Poseidons and four Trident D5s climbed into the upper atmosphere at exactly the same time, travelling at speeds of up to fifteen thousand miles per hour. Some were fired from silos buried deep under the ground. Some exploded out of specially adapted train carriages. Others came from submarines. And nobody knew who had given the order. It was a billion-dollar fireworks display that would change the world for ever.

And in ninety minutes it would all be over.

In the communications room the computer screens were flashing red. The entire operating board was ablaze with flashing lights. Cray stood up. There was a serene smile on his face.

"Well, that's it," he said. "There's nothing anyone can do now."

"They'll stop them!" Alex said. "As soon as they realize what's happened, they'll press a button and all your missiles will self-destruct."

"I'm afraid it's not quite as easy as that. You see, all the launch protocols have been obeyed. It was the Air Force One computer that set the missiles off; so only Air Force One can terminate them. I noticed you eyeing the little red button on the keyboard right here. SELF-DESTRUCT. But I'm afraid you're not going anywhere near it, Alex. We're leaving."

Cray gestured with the gun and Alex was forced out of the communications room and back down to the main cabin. His head was still hurting where

Cray had hit him. He needed to recover his strength. But how much time did he have left?

Yassen and Sabina were waiting for them. As soon as Alex appeared, Sabina tried to go over to him but Yassen held her back. Cray sank into a sofa next to her.

"Time to go!" he said. He smiled at Alex. "You realize, of course, that once this plane is in the air, it's virtually indestructible. You could say it's the perfect getaway vehicle. That's the beauty of it. It has over two hundred and thirty miles of wiring inside the frame which is designed to withstand even the pulse of a thermonuclear blast. Not that it would make any difference anyway. If they did manage to shoot us down, the missiles would still find their target. The world would still be saved!"

Alex tried to clear his head. He had to think straight.

There were just the five of them on the plane. Sabina, Yassen, Damian Cray and himself – with Henryk in the cockpit. Alex looked out of the main door. The ring of fake American soldiers was still in place. Even if anyone at the airport glanced their way, they would see nothing wrong. Not that that was likely to happen. The authorities must still be concentrating on the cloud of deadly nerve gas that didn't in fact exist.

Alex knew that if he was going to do anything – if there was anything he could do – it would have to happen before the plane left the ground. Cray was right. Once the plane was in the air, he would have no chance at all.

"Close the door, Mr Gregorovich," Cray commanded. "I think we should be on our way."

"Wait a minute!" Alex started to get to his feet but Cray signalled to him to sit down. The gun was in his hand. It was a Smith and Wesson .40, small and powerful with its three and a half inch barrel and square handgrip. Alex knew that it was extremely dangerous to fire a gun on a normal plane. Breaking a window or penetrating the outer skin would depressurize the cabin and make flight impossible. But this, of course, was Air Force One. This was not a normal plane.

"Stay exactly where you are," Cray said.

"Where are you taking us?" Sabina demanded. Cray was still sitting on the sofa next to her. He obviously thought it would be better to keep her and Alex apart. He reached out and ran a finger across her cheek. Sabina shuddered. She found him revolting and didn't care if he knew it. "We're going to Russia," he said.

"Russia?" Alex looked puzzled.

"A new life for me. And a return home for Mr Gregorovich." Cray licked his lips. "As a matter of fact, Mr Gregorovich will be something of a hero."

"I rather doubt that." Alex couldn't keep the scorn out of his voice.

"Oh yes. Heroin is smuggled into the country – I am told – in lead-lined coffins, and the border guards simply look the other way. Of course, they're paid. Corruption is everywhere. Drugs are ten times less expensive in Russia than they are in Europe and there are at least three and a half million addicts in Moscow and St Petersburg. Mr Gregorovich will be ending a problem that has almost brought his country to its knees, and I know that the president will be grateful. So you see, it looks as if the two of us are going to live happily ever after – which, I'm afraid, is more than can be said for you."

Yassen had closed the door. Alex watched as he pulled the lever down, locking it. "Doors to automatic," said Yassen.

There was a speaker system active in the plane. Everything that was said in the main cabin could be heard in the cockpit. And, sitting at the flight deck, Henryk flicked a switch so that his voice too could be heard throughout the plane.

"This is your captain speaking," he said. "Please fasten your seat belts and prepare for take-off." He was joking: a grisly parody of a real departure. "Thank you for flying with Cray Airlines. I hope you have a pleasant flight."

The engines started up. Out of the window Alex saw the soldiers scatter and run back to the trucks. Their work was done. They would leave the airport and make their way home to Amsterdam. He glanced at Sabina. She was sitting very still and he remembered that she was waiting for him to do something. *I know things... You have to leave everything to me*. That was what he had told her. How very hollow the words sounded now.

Air Force One was equipped with four huge engines. Alex heard them as they began to turn. They were about to leave! Desperately he looked around him: at the closed door with its white lever slanting down, at the stairway leading up towards the cockpit, at the low tables and neatly arranged line of magazines, at the trolley with its bottles and glasses. Cray was sitting with his legs slightly apart, the gun resting on his thigh. Yassen was still standing by the door. He had a second gun. It was in one of his pockets but Alex knew that the Russian could draw, aim and fire before he had time to blink. There were no other weapons in sight, nothing he could get his hands on. Hopeless.

The plane jerked and began to pull back from its stand. Alex looked out of the window again and saw something extraordinary. There was a vehicle parked next to the VIP building, not far from the plane. It was like a miniature tractor, with three carriages attached, loaded with plastic boxes. As Alex watched, it was suddenly blown away as if it had been made of paper. The carriages spun round and broke free. The tractor itself crashed onto its side and skidded across the tarmac.

It was the engines! Normally a plane of this size would have been towed to an open area out of harm's way before it began to taxi. Cray, of course, wasn't going to wait. Air Force One had been put into reverse thrust and the engines – with a thrust rating of over two hundred thousand pounds – were so powerful that they would blow away anything or anyone who came near. Now it was the turn of the VIP building itself. Windows shattered, the glass exploding inwards. A security man had come out and Alex saw him thrown back like a plastic soldier fired from an elastic band. A voice came through on the speakers inside the cabin. Henryk must have connected up the radio so that they could hear.

"This is air traffic control to Air Force One." This time it was a man's voice. "You have no clearance to taxi. Please stop immediately."

The stairs that they had climbed to board the plane toppled to one side, crashing onto the tarmac. The plane was moving more quickly now, backing out onto the main apron.

"This is air traffic control to Air Force One. We repeat: you have no clearance to taxi. Can you please state your intentions..."

They were out in the open, away from the VIP lounge. The main runway was behind them. The rest of the airport must have been almost a mile away. Inside the cockpit Henryk put the plane into forward thrust, and Alex felt the jolt and heard the whine of the engines as once again they began to move. Cray was humming to himself, his eyes vacant, lost in his own world. But the Smith and Wesson was still in his hand and Alex knew that the slightest movement would bring an instant response. Yassen hadn't stirred. He also seemed wrapped up in his own thoughts, as if he was trying to forget that this was happening.

The plane began to pick up speed, heading for the runway. There was a computer in the cockpit and Henryk had already fed in all the necessary information: the weight of the plane, the outside air temperature, the wind speed, the pressure. He would take off into the breeze, now coming from the east. The main runway is nearly four thousand metres long and the computer had already calculated that the aircraft would only need two and a half thousand of them. It was almost empty. This was going to be an easy take-off.

"Air Force One. You have no clearance. Please abort immediately. Repeat: abort at once."

The voice from air traffic control was still buzzing in his headphones. Henryk reached up and turned the radio off. He knew that an emergency overdrive would have gone into operation and any other planes would be diverted out of his way. After all, this aircraft did belong to the president of the United States of America. Already the Heathrow authorities would be screaming at each other over the phone lines, fearing not just a crash but a major diplomatic incident. Downing Street would have been informed. All over London, officials and civil servants would be asking the same desperate question.

What the hell is going on?

A hundred kilometres above their heads, the eight Peacekeeper missiles were nearing the edge of space. Two of their rockets had already burnt out and separated, leaving only the last sections with their deployment modules and protective shrouds. The Minutemen and the other missiles that Cray had fired weren't far behind. All of them carried top-secret and highly advanced navigation systems. On-board computers were already calculating trajectories and making adjustments. Soon the missiles would turn and lock into their targets.

And in eighty minutes they would fall back to earth.

Air Force One was moving rapidly now, following the taxi paths to the main runway. Ahead was the holding point where it would make a sharp turn and begin pre-flight checks.

In the cabin Sabina examined Cray as if seeing him for the first time. Her face showed only contempt. "I wonder what they'll do with you when you get to Russia," she said.

"What do you mean?" Cray asked.

"I wonder if they'll get rid of you by sending you back to England or just shoot you and be done with it."

Cray stared at her. He looked as if he had been slapped across the face. Alex flinched, fearing the worst. And it came.

"I've had enough of these guttersnipes," Cray snapped. "They're not amusing me any more." He turned to Yassen. "Kill them."

Yassen seemed not to have heard. "What?" he asked.

"You heard me. I'm bored of them. Kill them now!"

The plane stopped. They had reached the holding point. Henryk had heard the instructions being given in the main cabin but he ignored what was happening as he went through the final procedures: lifting the elevators up and down, turning the ailerons. He was seconds away from take-off. As soon as he was satisfied that the plane was ready, he would push down the four thrust levers and they would rocket forward. He tested the rudder pedals and the nose wheel. Everything was ready.

"I do not kill children," Yassen said. Alex had heard him say exactly the same thing on the boat in the South of France. He hadn't believed him then, but he wondered now what was going on inside the Russian's mind.

Sabina watched Alex intently, waiting for him to do something. But trapped inside the plane, with the whine of the engines already beginning to rise, there was nothing he could do. Not yet...

"What are you saying?" Cray demanded.

"There is no need for this," Yassen said. "Take them with us. They can do no harm."

"Why should I want to take them all the way to Russia?"

"We can lock them in one of the cabins. You don't even need to see them."

"Mr Gregorovich..." Cray was breathing heavily. There was a bead of sweat on his forehead and his grip on the gun was tighter than ever. "If you don't kill them, I will."

Yassen didn't move.

"All right! All right!" Cray sighed. "I thought I was meant to be in charge, but it seems that I have to do everything myself."

Cray brought up his gun. Alex got to his feet.

"No!" Sabina cried.

Cray fired.

But he hadn't been aiming at Sabina or even at Alex. The bullet hit Yassen in the chest, spinning him away from the door. "I'm sorry, Mr Gregorovich," he said. "But you're fired."

Then he turned the gun on Alex.

"You're next," he said.

He fired a second time.

Sabina cried out in horror. Cray had aimed at

Alex's heart, and in the confined space of the cabin there was little chance he could miss. The force of the bullet threw Alex off his feet and back across the cabin. He crashed to the ground and lay still.

Sabina threw herself at Cray. Alex was dead. The plane was taking off. Nothing mattered any more. Cray fired at her but the shot missed and suddenly she was right up against him, her hands clawing at his eyes, shouting all the time. But Cray was too strong for her. He brought an arm round, grabbed hold of her and threw her back against the door. She lay there, dazed and help-less. The gun came up.

"Goodbye, my dear," Cray said.

He aimed. But before he could fire, his arm was seized from behind. Sabina stared. Alex was up again and he was unhurt. It was impossible. But, like Cray, she had no way of knowing that he was wearing the bulletproof jersey that Smithers had given him with the bike. The bullet had hurt him; he thought it might have cracked a rib. But although it had knocked him down, it hadn't penetrated his skin.

Now Alex was on top of Cray. The man was small – only a little taller than Alex himself – but even so he was thickset and surprisingly strong.

Alex managed to get one hand around Cray's wrist, keeping the gun away from him. But Cray's other hand grabbed Alex's neck, his fingers curling into the side of Alex's throat.

"Sabina! Get out of here!" Alex managed to shout the words before his air supply was cut off. The gun was out of control. He was using all his strength to stop Cray from aiming it at him and he wasn't sure how much longer he would be able to hold him off. Sabina ran over to the main door and pulled up the white handle to open it.

At that exact moment, in the cockpit, Henryk pushed the four thrust levers all the way down. From where he sat, the runway stretched out in front of him. The path was clear. Air Force One lurched forward and started to take off.

The main door flew open with a loud hiss. It had been set to automatic before the plane began to move, and as soon as Sabina had unlocked it, a pneumatic system had kicked in. An orange slide extended itself from the doorway like a giant tongue and began to inflate. The emergency slide.

Wind and dust rushed in, a miniature tornado that whirled madly through the cabin. Cray had brought the gun round, aiming at Alex's head, but the force of the wind surprised him. The magazines on the table flew into the air, flapping into his face like giant moths. The trolley of drinks broke loose and rattled across the carpet, bottles and glasses crashing down.

Cray's face was contorted, his perfect teeth in a twisted snarl, his eyes bulging. He swore, but no sound could be heard against the roar of the engines. Sabina was pressed against the wall, staring helplessly through the open doorway at the grass and concrete rushing past in a green and grey blur. Yassen wasn't moving; blood was spreading slowly across his shirt. Alex could feel the strength draining out of him. He relaxed his grip and the gun went off. Sabina screamed. The bullet had smashed a light fitting inches from her face. Alex jabbed down, trying to knock the gun out of Cray's hand. Cray slammed a knee into his stomach and Alex reeled back, gasping for breath. The plane continued, faster and faster, hurtling down the runway.

Behind the controls Henryk was suddenly sweating. The eyes behind the spectacles were confused. He had seen a light blink on, warning him that a door had opened and that the main cabin was depressurized. He was already travelling at a hundred and thirty miles an hour. Air traffic control must have realized what was happening and would have alerted the authorities.

If he stopped now, he would be arrested. But did he dare take off?

And then the on-board computer spoke.

"V1..."

It was a machine voice. Utterly emotionless. Two syllables brought together by electronic circuitry. And they were the last two syllables Henryk wanted to hear.

Normally it would have been the first officer who called out the speeds, keeping an eye on the progress of the plane. But Henryk was on his own. He had to rely on the automated system. What the computer was telling him was that the plane was moving at one hundred and fifty miles per hour – V1 – decision speed. He was now going too fast to stop. If he tried to abort the take-off, if he put the engines into reverse, he would crash.

It is the moment every pilot dreads – and the single most dangerous moment in any flight. More plane crashes have been caused by a wrong decision at this time than by anything else. Every instinct in Henryk's body told him to stop. He was safe on the ground. A crash here would be better than a crash from fifteen hundred feet up in the air. But if he did try to stop, a crash would be the certain result.

He didn't know what to do.

                    *   *   *

The sun was setting in the town of Quetta in Pakistan, but life in the refugee camp was as busy as ever. Hundreds of people clutching blankets and stoves made their way through a miniature city of tents, while children, some of them in rags, queued for vaccinations. A row of women sat on benches, working on a quilt, beating and folding the cotton.

The air was cool and fresh in the Patkai Hills of Myanmar, the country that had once been Burma. Fourteen hundred metres above sea level, the breeze carried the scent of pine trees and flowers. It was half past nine at night and most people were asleep. A few shepherds sat alone with their flocks. Thousands of stars littered the night sky.

In Colombia, in the Urabá region, another day had dawned and the smell of chocolate wafted down the village street. The *campesinas* – the farmers' wives – had begun working at dawn, toasting the cacao beans, then splitting the shells. Children were drawn to their doors, taking in the rich, irresistible scent.

And in the highlands of Peru, north of Arequipa, families in colourful clothes made their way to the markets, some carrying the little bundles of fruit and vegetables that were all they had to sell. A woman in a bowler hat sat hunched up beside a row of sacks, each one filled with a different spice. Laughing teenagers kicked a football in the street.

These were the targets that the missiles had selected, far out in space. There were thousands – millions – more like them. And they were all innocent. They knew about the fields where the poppies were grown. They knew the men who worked there. But that was no concern of theirs. Life had to go on.

And none of them had any knowledge of the deadly missiles that were already closing in on them. None of them saw the horror that was coming their way.

The end came very quickly on Air Force One.

Cray was punching the side of Alex's head again and again. Alex still clung to the gun, but his grip was weakening. He finally fell back, bloody and exhausted. His face was bruised, his eyes half closed.

The emergency slide was jutting out now, horizontal with the plane. The rush of air was pushing it back, slanting it towards the wings. The plane was travelling at a hundred and eighty miles per hour. It would leave the ground in less than ten seconds' time.

Cray raised the gun one last time.

Then he cried out as something slammed into him. It was Sabina. She had grabbed hold of the trolley and used it as a battering ram. The trolley hit him behind the knees. His legs buckled and he lost his balance, toppling over backwards. He landed on top of the trolley, dropping the gun. Sabina dived for it, determined that he wouldn't fire another shot.

And that was when Alex rose up.

He had quickly gauged distances and angles. He knew what he had to do. With a cry he threw himself forward, his arms outstretched. His palms slammed into the side of the trolley. Cray yelled out. The trolley shot across the main area of the cabin and, with Cray still on top of it, out the door.

And it didn't stop there. The emergency slide slanted gently towards the ground that was shooting past far below. It was held in place by the rushing wind and by the compressed air inside it. The trolley bounced out onto the slide and began to roll down. Alex staggered over to the door just in time to see Cray begin his fairground ride to hell. The slide carried him halfway down, the force of the wind tilting him back towards the wings.

Damian Cray came into the general area of engine two.

The last thing he saw was the engine's gaping mouth. Then the wind rush took him. With a dreadful, inaudible scream he was pulled into the engine. The trolley went with him.

Cray was mincemeat. More than that, he was vaporized. In one second he had been turned into a cloud of red gas that disappeared into the atmosphere. There was simply nothing left. But the metal trolley offered more resistance. There was a bang like a cannon shot. A huge tongue of flame exploded out of the back as the engine was torn apart.

That was when the plane went out of control.

Henryk had decided to abort take-off and was trying to slow down, but now it was too late. An engine on one side had suddenly stopped. Both engines on the other side were still on full power. The imbalance sent the plane lurching violently to the left. Alex and Sabina were thrown to the floor. Lights fused and sparked all around them. Anything that wasn't securely fastened whirled through the air. Henryk fought for control but it was hopeless. The plane veered away and left the runway. That was the end of it. The soft ground was unable to support such a huge load. With a terrible shearing of metal, the undercarriage broke off and the whole thing toppled over onto one side.

The entire cabin twisted round and Alex felt the floor tilt beneath his feet. It was as if the plane was turning upside down. But finally it stopped. The engines cut out. The plane rested on its side and the scream of sirens filled the air as emergency vehicles raced across the tarmac.

Alex tried to move but his legs wouldn't obey him. He was lying on the floor and he could feel the darkness closing in. But he knew he had to stay conscious. His work wasn't finished yet.

"Sab?" He called out to her and was relieved when she got to her feet and came over.

"Alex?"

"You have to get to the communications room. There's a button. Self-destruct." For a moment she looked blank and he took hold of her arm. "The missiles..."

"Yes. Yes ... of course." She was in shock. Too much had happened. But she understood. She staggered up the stairs, balancing herself against the sloping walls. Alex lay where he was.

And then Yassen spoke.

"Alex..."

Alex didn't have enough strength left to be surprised. He turned his head slowly, expecting to see a gun in the Russian's hand. It didn't seem fair to him. After so much, was he really going to die now, just when help was on its way? But Yassen wasn't holding a gun. He had propped himself up against a table. He was covered in blood now and there was a strange quality to his eyes as the blue slowly drained out. Yassen's skin was even paler than usual and, as his head tilted back, Alex noticed for the first time that he had a long scar on his neck. It was dead straight, as if it had been drawn with a ruler.

"Please..." Yassen's voice was soft.

It was the last thing he wanted to do, but Alex crawled through the wreckage of the cabin and over to him. He remembered that Cray's death and the destruction of the plane had only happened because Yassen had refused to kill Sabina and him.

"What happened to Cray?" Yassen asked.

"He went off his trolley," Alex said.

"He's dead?"

"Very."

Yassen nodded, as if pleased. "I knew it was a mistake working for him," he said. "I knew." He fought for breath, narrowing his eyes for a moment. "There is something I have to tell you, Alex," he said. The strange thing was that he was speaking absolutely normally, as if this were a quiet conversation between friends. Despite himself, Alex found himself marvelling at the man's self-control. He must have only minutes to live.

Then Yassen spoke again and everything in Alex's life changed for ever.

"I couldn't kill you," he said. "I would never have killed you. Because, you see, Alex ... I knew your father."

"What?" Despite his exhaustion, despite all the pain from his injuries, Alex felt something shiver through him.

"Your father. He and I..." Yassen had to catch his breath. "We worked together."

"He worked with you?"

"Yes."

"You mean ... he was a spy?"

"Not a spy, no, Alex. He was a killer. Like me. He was the very best. The best in the world. I knew him when I was nineteen. He taught me many things..."

"No!" Alex refused to accept what he was hearing. He had never met his father, knew nothing about him. But what Yassen was saying couldn't be true. It was some sort of horrible trick.

The sirens were getting nearer. The first of the vehicles must have arrived. He could hear men shouting outside.

"I don't believe you," Alex cried. "My father wasn't a killer. He couldn't have been!"

"I'm telling you the truth. You have to know."

"Did he work for MI6?"

"No." The ghost of a smile flickered across Yassen's face. But it was filled with sadness. "MI6 hunted him down. They killed him. They tried to kill both of us. At the last minute I escaped, but he..." Yassen swallowed. "They killed your father, Alex."

"No!"

"Why would I lie to you?" Yassen reached out weakly and took hold of Alex's arm. It was the first physical contact the two had ever had. "Your father ... he did this." Yassen drew a finger along the scar on his neck, but his voice was failing him and he couldn't explain. "He saved my life. In a way, I loved him. I love you too, Alex. You are so very much like him. I'm glad that you're here with me now." There was a pause and a spasm of pain rippled across the dying man's face. There was one last thing he had to say. "If you don't believe me, go to Venice. Find Scorpia. And you will find your destiny..."

Yassen shut his eyes and Alex knew he would never open them again.

In the communications room Sabina found the button and pressed it. In space the first of the Minutemen blew itself into thousands of pieces, a brilliant, soundless explosion. Seconds later the other missiles did the same.

Air Force One was surrounded. A fleet of emergency vehicles had reached it and two trucks were spraying it down, covering it in torrents of white foam.

But Alex didn't know any of this. He was lying next to Yassen, his eyes closed. He had quietly and thankfully passed out.

RICHMOND BRIDGE

The swans really weren't going anywhere. They seemed happy just to circle slowly in the sunshine, occasionally dipping their beaks under the surface of the water, searching for insects, algae, whatever. Alex had been watching them for the last half-hour, almost hypnotized by them. He wondered what it was like to be a swan. He wondered how they managed to keep their feathers so white.

He was sitting on a bench beside the Thames, just outside Richmond. This was where the river seemed to abandon London, finally leaving the city behind it on the other side of Richmond Bridge. Looking upstream, Alex could see fields and woodland, absurdly green, sprawled out in the heat of the English summer.

An au pair, pushing a pram, walked past on the towpath. She noticed Alex, and although her expression didn't change, her hands tightened on the pram and she very slightly quickened her pace. Alex knew that he looked terrible, like something out of one of those posters put out by the local council. Alex Rider, fourteen, in need of fostering. His last fight with Damian Cray had left its marks. But this time it was more than cuts and bruises. They would fade like others had faded before. This time he had seen his whole life bend out of shape.

He couldn't stop thinking about Yassen Gregorovich. Two weeks had gone by but he was still waking up in the middle of the night, reliving the final moments on Air Force One. His father had been a contract killer, murdered by the very people who had now taken over his own life. It couldn't be true. Yassen must have been lying, trying to wound Alex in revenge for what had happened between them. Alex wanted to believe it. But he had looked into the dying man's eyes and had seen no deceit, only a strange sort of tenderness – and a desire for the truth to be known.

Go to Venice. Find Scorpia. Find your destiny...

It seemed to Alex that his only destiny was to be lied to and manipulated by adults who cared nothing about him. Should he go to Venice? How would he find Scorpia? For that matter, was Scorpia a person or a place? Alex watched the swans, wishing they could give him an answer. But they just drifted on the water, ignoring him.

A shadow fell across the bench. Alex looked up and felt a fist close tightly inside his stomach. Mrs Jones was standing over him. The MI6 agent was dressed in grey silk trousers with a matching jacket that hung down to her knees, almost like a coat. There was a silver pin in her lapel but no other jewellery. It seemed strange for her to be out here, in the sun. He didn't want to see her. Along with Alan Blunt, she was the last person Alex wanted to see.

"May I join you?" she asked.

"It seems you already have," Alex said.

She sat down next to him.

"Have you been following me?" Alex asked. He wondered how she had known he would be here and it occurred to him that he might have been under round-the-clock surveillance for the past fortnight. It wouldn't have surprised him.

"No. Your friend – Jack Starbright – told me you'd be here."

"I'm meeting someone."

"Not until twelve. Jack came in to see me,

Alex. You should have reported to Liverpool Street by now. We need to debrief you."

"There's no point reporting to Liverpool Street," Alex said bitterly. "There's nothing there, is there? Just a bank."

Mrs Jones understood. "That was wrong of us," she said.

Alex turned away.

"I know you don't want to talk to me, Alex," Mrs Jones continued. "Well, you don't have to. But will you please just listen?"

She looked anxiously at him. He said nothing. She went on.

"It's true that we didn't believe you when you came to us – and of course we were wrong. We were stupid. But it just seemed so incredible that a man like Damian Cray could be a threat to national security. He was rich and he was eccentric; nevertheless, he was only a pop star with attitude. That was what we thought.

"But if you think we ignored you completely, Alex, you're wrong. Alan and I have different ideas about you. To be honest, if it had been my choice, we'd never have got you involved in the first place ... not even in that business with the Stormbreakers. But that's not the issue here." She took a deep breath. "After you had gone,

I decided to take another look at Damian Cray. There wasn't a great deal I could do without the right authority, but I had him watched and all his movements were reported back to me.

"I heard you were at Hyde Park, in that dome when the Gameslayer was launched. I also got a police report on the woman – the journalist – who was killed. It just seemed like an unfortunate coincidence. Then I was told there had been an incident in Paris: a photographer and his assistant killed. Meanwhile Damian Cray was in Holland, and the next thing I knew, the Dutch police were screaming about some sort of high-speed chase in Amsterdam: cars and motorbikes chasing a boy on a bicycle. Of course, I knew it was you. But I still had no idea what was going on.

"And then your friend, Sabina, disappeared at Whitchurch Hospital. That really got the alarm bells ringing. I know. You're probably thinking we were absurdly slow, and you're right. But every intelligence service in the world is the same. When they act, they're efficient. But often they get started too late.

"That was the case here. By the time we came to bring you in, you were already with Cray, in Wiltshire. We spoke to your housekeeper, Jack. Then we went straight to his house. But we missed you again and this time we had no idea where you'd gone. Now we know, of course. Air Force One! The CIA have been going crazy. Alan Blunt was called in to see the prime minister last week. It may well be that he is forced to resign."

"Well, that breaks my heart," Alex said.

Mrs Jones ignored this. "Alex ... what you've been through ... I know this has been very difficult for you. You were on your own, and that should never have happened. But the fact is, you have saved millions of lives. Whatever you're feeling now, you have to remember that. It might even be true to say that you saved the world. God knows what the consequences would have been if Cray had succeeded. Anyway, the president of the United States would very much like to meet you. So, for that matter, would the prime minister. And for what it's worth, you've even been invited to the Palace, if you want to go. Of course, nobody else knows about you. You're still classified. But you should be proud of yourself. What you did was ... amazing."

"What happened to Henryk?" Alex asked. The question took Mrs Jones by surprise, but it was the only thing he didn't know. "I just wondered," he said.

"He's dead," Mrs Jones said. "He was killed

when the plane crashed. He broke his neck."

"Well, that's that then." Alex turned to her. "Can you go now?"

"Jack is worried about you, Alex. So am I. It may be that you need help coming to terms with what happened. Maybe some sort of therapy."

"I don't want therapy. I just want to be left alone."

"All right."

Mrs Jones stood up. She made one last attempt to read him before she left. This was the fourth occasion she had met Alex at the end of an assignment. Each time she had known that he must have been, in some way, damaged. But this time something worse had happened. She knew there was something Alex wasn't telling her.

And then, on an impulse, she said, "You were on the plane with Yassen when he was shot. Did he say anything before he died?"

"What do you mean?"

"Did he talk to you?"

Alex looked her straight in the eye. "No. He never spoke."

Alex watched her leave. So it was true what Yassen had said. Her last question had proved it. He knew who he was.

The son of a contract killer.

* * *

Sabina was waiting for him under the bridge. He knew that this was going to be a brief meeting. There was nothing really left to say.

"How are you?" she asked.

"I'm OK. How's your dad?"

"He's a lot better." She shrugged. "I think he's going to be fine."

"And he's not going to change his mind?"

"No, Alex. We're leaving."

Sabina had told him on the phone the night before. She and her parents were leaving the country. They wanted to be on their own, to give her father time to recover fully. They had decided it would be easier for him to begin a new life and had chosen San Francisco. Edward had been offered a job by a big newspaper there. And there was more good news. He was writing a book: the truth about Damian Cray. It was going to make him a fortune.

"When do you go?" Alex asked.

"Tuesday." Sabina brushed something out of her eye and Alex wondered if it might have been a tear. But when she looked at him again, she was smiling. "Of course, we'll keep in touch," she said. "We can email. And you know you can always come out if you want a holiday."

"As long as it's not like the last one," Alex said.

"It'll be weird going to an American school..." Sabina broke off. "You were fantastic on the plane, Alex," she said suddenly. "I couldn't believe how brave you were. When Cray was telling you all those crazy things, you didn't even seem scared of him." She stopped. "Will you work for MI6 again?" she asked.

"No."

"Do you think they'll leave you alone?"

"I don't know, Sabina. It was my uncle's fault, really. He started all this years ago and now I'm stuck with it."

"I still feel ashamed about not believing you." Sabina sighed. "And I understand now what you must have been going through. They made me sign the Official Secrets Act. I'm not allowed to tell anyone about you." A pause. "I'll never forget you," she said.

"I'll miss you, Sabina."

"But we'll see each other again. You can come to California. And I'll let you know if I'm ever in London..."

"That's good."

She was lying. Somehow Alex knew that this was more than goodbye, that the two of them would never see each other again. There was no reason for it. That was just the way it was going to be.

She put her arms around him and kissed him.

"Goodbye, Alex," she said.

He watched her walk out of his life. Then he turned and followed the river, past the swans and off into the countryside. He didn't stop. Nor did he look back.

STORMBREAKER
Anthony Horowitz

Meet Alex Rider, the reluctant teenage spy.

When his guardian dies in suspicious circum-stances, fourteen-year-old Alex Rider finds his world turned upside down.

Within days he's gone from schoolboy to superspy. Forcibly recruited into MI6, Alex has to take part in gruelling SAS training exercises. Then, armed with his own special set of secret gadgets, he's off on his first mission.

His destination is the depths of Cornwall, where Middle-Eastern multimillionaire Herod Sayle is producing his state-of-the-art Stormbreaker com-puters. Sayle's offered to give one free to every school in the country – but MI6 think there's more to the gift than meets the eye.

Only Alex can find out the truth. But time is run-ning out and Alex soon finds himself in mortal danger. It looks as if his first assignment may well be his last...

Explosive, thrilling, action-packed, *Stormbreaker* reveals Anthony Horowitz at his brilliant best.

"Is there anybody in Britain who will not enjoy this fabulous junior James Bond adventure?"
The Daily Mail

"The perfect hero ... genuine 21st century stuff."
The Daily Telegraph

POINT BLANC
Anthony Horowitz

Alex Rider, teenage superspy, is back!

Fourteen-year-old Alex Rider, reluctant MI6 spy, is back at school trying to adapt to his new double life ... and to double homework.

But MI6 have other plans for him.

Investigations into the "accidental" deaths of two of the world's most powerful men have revealed just one link. Both had a son attending Point Blanc Academy – an exclusive school for rebellious rich kids, run by the sinister Dr Grief and set high on an isolated mountain peak in the French Alps.

Armed only with a false ID and a new collection of brilliantly disguised gadgets, Alex must infiltrate the academy as a pupil and establish the truth about what is really happening there. Can he alert the world to what he discovers before it is too late?

"Horowitz will grip you with suspense, daring and cheek – and that's just the first page! Prepare for action scenes as fast as a movie. A stormin' follow-up to *Stormbreaker*." *The Times*

"A hugely entertaining, fast-paced book which more than deserves five stars."
www.cool-reads.co.uk

SKELETON KEY
Anthony Horowitz

Sharks. Assassins. Nuclear bombs. Alex Rider's in deep water.

Reluctant teenage superspy Alex Rider is useful to MI6 in ways an adult could never be. Now they need his help once again.

But a routine reconnaissance mission at the Wimbledon Tennis Championships sets off a terrifying chain of events for Alex that sees him on the run from a murderous Chinese triad gang. Forced to hide out, Alex is sent to Cayo Esqueleto – Skeleton Key – an island near Cuba. Waiting for him there is General Alexei Sarov – a coldly insane Russian with explosive plans to rewrite history.

Alex faces his most dangerous challenge yet. Alone, and equipped only with a handful of ingenious gadgets, Alex must outwit Sarov, as the seconds tick away towards the end of the world...

"Brings new meaning to the phrase *action-packed*." *The Sunday Times*

"Every bored schoolboy's fantasy, only a thousand times funnier, slicker and more exciting ... genius." *The Independent on Sunday*

GROOSHAM GRANGE
Anthony Horowitz

New pupils are made to sign their names in blood...

The assistant headmaster has no reflection...

The French teacher disappears whenever there's a full moon...

Groosham Grange, David Eliot's new school, is a very weird place indeed!

"One of the funniest books of the year." *Young Telegraph*

"Hilarious ... speeds along at full tilt from page to page." *Books for Keeps*

RETURN TO GROOSHAM GRANGE
Anthony Horowitz

A year ago, David Eliot would have been happy to escape from his weird school and its ghoulish teachers. Now he's fighting for its survival. Someone is trying to get their hands on the Unholy Grail, the source of all power, and unless David can stop them, Groosham Grange will be history!

"A first-class children's novelist."
The Times Educational Supplement

"Horowitz has become a writer who converts boys to reading." *The Times*

THE FALCON'S MALTESER
Anthony Horowitz

"Johnny Naples opened his mouth and tried to speak. 'The falcon...' he said. Then a nasty, bubbling sound."

When vertically challenged Johnny Naples entrusts Tim Diamond with a package worth over three million pounds, he's making a big mistake. For Tim Diamond is probably the worst detective in the entire world. Next day, Johnny's dead. Tim gets the blame, his smart, wisecracking younger brother Nick gets the package – and every crook in town is out to get them!

"Any child with a quick sense of humour should love it... An abundance of jokes, most of them first-class." *The Times Literary Supplement*

SOUTH BY SOUTH EAST
Anthony Horowitz

"McGuffin had finished talking. The telephone was dead and any minute now he'd be joining it. The stuff he had spilled down the coat was blood, his own blood…"

Tim Diamond, the world's worst private detective, is broke – as his much smarter younger brother Nick is quick to remind him. So, when a mysterious stranger offers Tim a wad of money for his overcoat, it seems like a stroke of good luck. But there are worse things in life than being broke. Being pumped full of lead for one – which is what happens to the stranger and could soon be the fate of the Diamond brothers too, unless they can outwit the unknown assassin on their tail!

PUBLIC ENEMY NUMBER TWO
Anthony Horowitz

"So there I was in a maximum-security prison out-side London, accused of theft, trespass, criminal damage and cruelty to animals... Me ... public enemy number two!"

Framed for a jewel robbery, quick-thinking young Nick Diamond finds himself sharing a prison cell with Johnny Powers, Public Enemy Number One. His only chance of rescuing the situation is to nail the Fence, the country's master criminal. First, though, Nick has to get out of jail – which is where his older brother Tim, the world's worst private detective, comes in... But with Ma Powers and her gang waiting to greet the jailbirds, the heat is really on for the Diamond brothers in this explosive adventure!

THE BLURRED MAN
Anthony Horowitz

"'My name is Carter,' he said at last. He spoke with an American accent. 'Joe Carter. I've just got in from Chicago. And I've got a problem.'"

The man in the photo is so blurry, it's impossible to make out what he really looks like. And that's before he was run over by a steamroller! His name was Lenny Smile and he ran a children's charity called Dream Time, financed by millionaire author Joe Carter. Now Carter wants to know just what happened to Smile – and to the money. Unfortunately for him, he's hired the Diamond brothers – Tim, the world's worst private detective, and his wisecracking younger brother Nick – to solve the mystery!

THE FRENCH CONFECTION
Anthony Horowitz

"'Tim,' I asked. 'What's the French for "murder"?'
Tim shrugged. 'Why do you want to know?' 'I don't
know.' I stepped onto the escalator and let it carry
me down. 'I've just got a feeling it's something
we're going to need.'"

When the hard-up Diamond brothers, Tim and Nick,
win a weekend for two in Paris, it looks as if their
luck is taking a turn for the better. But looks can
be deceptive. No sooner have they arrived in the
French capital than the brothers are up to their
necks in danger. There's a nasty smell in the air and
it's not the cheese. If Nick and Tim aren't careful,
their dream holiday could end up being a nightmare from which they'll never wake...

I KNOW WHAT YOU DID LAST WEDNESDAY
Anthony Horowitz

"It's not fair. I do my homework. I clean my teeth twice a day. Why does everyone want to kill me?"

It's a dangerous life being the younger brother of the world's worst private detective – but Nick Diamond's survived ... so far. He's due a holiday, so he should be happy when an invitation arrives for his brother Tim inviting him to a school reunion on a remote Scottish island – and offering to pay him for the pleasure. But Nick's got a bad feeling and it's not indigestion. And when he meets their fellow guests, the feeling only gets worse – especially when they start dying in ever more bizarre ways! Could it be the Diamond brothers' days are numbered?